Will Rafe find a way to confront his past?

Rafe walked into the field, pushing his way through the high weeds until he came to the remains of an old cabin. Now to find the exact place where he had first come into the 1990s, a weeping little boy of seven who thought he had lost his mother forever.

Where could it be? Down in that creek bed? Rafe climbed down into it, putting his hands out in front of him to break his fall in case he tripped.

One hand disappeared in front of his eyes. He jabbed the other arm farther out—and that one vanished up to the elbow.

Now he squatted down. Cautiously, ever so cautiously, he leaned into—

"There he be!" someone cried.

He saw a rifle being yanked up to firing level by a running man, saw the flash before he heard the shot. A burning whisper of death singed his ear, leaving the smell of gunpowder.

"Don't you move, little slave boy! Lessen you'd sooner be dead than go back to your master! Get him! Get him!"

Return to
GHOST HOTEL

Larry Weinberg

Troll

To the memory of my mother,
who speaks to me still.

ONE

The fight in the school yard started when another black kid said to Rafe, "You made up all that stuff you said in social studies 'bout Mother Freedom, didn't you?"

"No, I didn't. Slaves down South in Kentucky called her that because she helped a lot of them get to the North. Then other people in the Underground Railroad helped to smuggle them up to Canada so they wouldn't be sent back."

"Uh-huh. And then you said her real name was Rosalie Sims."

"So?"

"Well, Sims, that's *your* name."

"What about it?"

"You want everybody to believe that this Mother Freedom who nobody else ever heard of—"

"Hold on. There's plenty of people who are *gonna* hear about her, because Mr. Post is writing a book on her."

"Who? You mean that white man whose family you live with?"

Rafe didn't like the way William had sneered the word *white*—as if there was something wrong with his staying with anybody who wasn't African-American. "That's right," he shot back. "His great-great-grandfolks were part of the Underground Railroad up here in Rochester. They took runaways from Harriet Tubman and Sojourner Truth and slipped them over the border into Canada. And before she was killed, they all knew about my—"

Rafe stopped himself before the next word flew out of his mouth. But then he thought about it—about how much he really wanted to say it. He looked up smiling, and slowly he said, "All about my mother."

William bent low over the much smaller youngster. "Your what? Your *mother*? Man, that was like a hundred years ago."

"No," said the boy pleasantly. "It was more like a hundred and fifty."

"Oh. You're over a hundred and fifty years old."

"Not exactly, because then I'd be a long time dead. I'm closer to ten years old."

"Explain that one to me, boy. I'd really like to hear it."

"No problem, William. One night when I was seven, there were slave catchers with rifles chasing after me, and—"

"Oh, you was a slave."

"That's what I'm trying to tell you. But I took a jump through time to get away. That's how come I'm here talking to you."

"Uh-huh. And what happened to Mother Freedom?"

The little grin left Rafe's face. "They shot her and then they hanged her."

"How come they didn't just shoot her again if she was only wounded?"

"No, she was already dead, all right," said Rafe. He was getting really upset. "But they hated her so much, they hanged her anyway."

A smoky fire had started in his eyes. William stared at him. "Man, you *believe* this?"

"No, I'm lying," Rafe snapped as his hands began to curl.

8

He was starting not to care anymore who'd get the worst of a fight.

William stared down at those tiny fists. They only made him grin. "You say you're lying, but I see you're about to bust. And I just think you're crazy."

"Yeah, that's me, *crazy*. But don't let that stop you from swinging at me, William."

"Oh? Why's that?"

"'Cause I've been wanting to hit somebody back for a long time."

"Suits me fine," said William, poking him hard enough in the chest to send him falling back against the chain-link fence. "You're just about to get your chance!"

The call from the vice principal was picked up by fifteen-year-old Anna Post. She took the call in her room, where she was lying down, nursing the cold that had kept her home that day. Perhaps it was her scratchy voice that made her sound old enough to be mistaken for Mrs. Post.

The vice principal was very sorry to report that Rafe was being suspended for the rest of this week for fighting. He'd had to be treated by the nurse for a split lip and a bloody nose and a puffed-up eye. But he'd been so "wildly violent" that he'd managed to beat up a boy almost twice his size. Right now he was not being allowed to return to class. Would someone drive down to pick him up or must they keep him in the office until after school?

"Hold him for the bus, if you don't mind," said Anna, in her deepest voice. "My husband has the car." She paused, then added, "But I must say that if Rafe was in a fight, he certainly was not the one who started it. He does not look for trouble. And he is a very fine student."

"A good student? Well, yes and no," mused the vice principal absently. "He does get good grades because he's bright and can coast along. But lately he really doesn't pay attention. He mopes around. He fidgets. And if and when he does say anything, it's usually to contradict the teacher. He seems to be resentful of something—or everything. His teacher has the feeling that Rafe is carrying a big chip on his shoulder, and that he finally found the right boy to knock it off."

"I must tell you," said Anna gravely, "this does not sound like our Rafe."

"Well, Mrs. Post, there's something else that I'd like to mention, now that we're discussing him. We've been waiting for two whole years to get the records from the last school he attended. Your husband promised to take care of that."

"Yes, that's my Allan for you," said Anna, imitating her mother's hopeless sigh. "Honestly, he is *so* absent-minded. I thought he already had."

"No, and in fact we don't even have a letter in the file from this boy's parents. I can't tell you how important it is that we see legal permission for Rafe Sims to be living with your family or even to be attending school in this district."

"I blame this on myself," said Anna. "My husband writes books, you see. And book writers live inside the world that's in their own minds. They have no idea of anything going on around them. But now you may rest assured that I will take care of this personally. Well, thank you for calling."

"No, wait a minute, please!" the vice principal said hastily. "Now this is very difficult for me, but I must tell you that Rafe has been sitting in my office for the last half hour insisting to anyone who walks in that he was born before the Civil War, and that he was a slave. He also says his mother freed slaves and was one of the leaders of the Underground Railroad."

"What? Why, that little stinker!" cried Anna in a voice that suddenly was very much her own.

"Just a minute. Is this *Mrs.* Post? Who am I speaking to?"

"Er, well, this is her daughter Anna. My mother . . . uh . . . had a fainting spell . . . and I took the phone. But she says you can talk to me. I'm very mature for my age."

There was a long pause, then the vice principal began again. "I was saying that he seems to be having a very serious identity problem. Do you know what that means?"

"Absolutely. I mean, that's a big teenage thing, right?"

"Well, at nine and a half, Rafe is certainly not a teenager. We think this identity problem may have something to do with his living with a . . . well, a family that's not of his own—"

"Of his own *race?* Well, ma'am, in our home we like to think of Rafe and ourselves as belonging to the *human* race."

"Oh, I didn't mean—well, so do I. Oh, dear, I do think I may be saying this badly . . ."

"No, it's all right. But you see," said Anna, launching into the family's long-thought-out cover story, "Rafe's mother is dead and he has no uncles or aunts. His father and my father saved each other's lives in Vietnam, and they're very close friends. Since Mr. Sims is always traveling around the world on business, his son is staying with us."

"Yes, yes, so we've been *told* in the past, but we don't have that in *writing* from Mr. Sims. And what we *do* have at the moment is a boy who actually seems to believe he's a traveler through time who came here out of the past. Children do get fanciful at times, I admit, but still, we have to be watchful of these things. I've just had a long discussion with our social worker and the school psychologist, as well as with Rafe's teacher. It really seems to us that before he returns to class after the Easter break he should be seen by a . . . well, a . . ."

"Psychiatrist?"

There was a pause. "Something like that, yes."

"I'll tell that to my parents when they come home. Thank you."

"Wait a minute! I thought you said your mother was right there."

"As soon as you started talking about looney-tune doctors, she had to go out for air!"

"Now listen here. You are twisting—"

"Bye."

Anna slammed the phone down, crying, "Oh, Rafe, you dummy! Wait till I get my hands on you!"

She was still fuming when the front door finally flew open. Her little brother Kevin bounded inside, grinning madly. "Hey, Anna, Rafe's been in a big fight! And he's broken his promise and told everybody—"

"I know that already! Stop gloating."

"I'm not gloating! What's gloating?"

"It's being happy that someone else is in a mess."

"Well, he did it to himself!"

"What does that matter, if you care about him? Or don't you?"

"Well, why should I when he's been so mean lately? It's

12

like he's been wanting *me* to fight with him, only I wouldn't do it."

"Didn't he come back with you? Where is he?"

Kevin's grin returned, and he jerked his thumb toward the door. "Still down by the bus stop. He's staying outside because he knows what's going to happen to him when you get hold of him. How's your cold?"

"My cold is terrific," she said, barging through the door. "That's why I'm going out in the rain."

She found Rafe giving all his attention to kicking at a puddle in the gutter. "You really went and did it this time, didn't you?" Anna said.

"Don't come down on my case, girl," Rafe grumbled.

"Why? Are you going to hit me, too?"

Rafe shrugged and splashed harder. Though his face was half turned from her, she could see he looked awful. It wasn't the greenish eye and swollen lip so much as that terribly lost expression he wore. Rafe seemed angry and sorry and hurt, all at the same time.

Anna's heart melted at once. It always did when he was unhappy. "Mom and Dad aren't home yet. Want to come inside where it's dry, and we'll talk it over?"

He shook his head.

"Why not?" she asked softly.

Rafe didn't answer. That was no surprise. Anna already knew that whenever Rafe was miserable he pushed people away and wanted to be by himself.

There was a chill to that early-spring rain. She had to clear her throat before she said softly but firmly, "Look, we've got to talk. Okay to walk?"

He nodded but didn't say anything as they turned the

corner and headed down the avenue. In silence they watched a few cars scatter puddles. Finally Anna said, "I want to know if you told them anything about me—about my coming from the past too."

Rafe shrugged.

"What does that mean?"

"It means," he mumbled, "that I don't remember."

That was a blow to her kindliness. Of course he remembered. "Don't fool around," she said between gritted teeth, trying to hold on to her good feelings about him. "Just tell me if you said anything about me, and I won't be mad."

"Why don't you ask Kevin?" Rafe snorted. "He loves to tell on me anyway."

It was easy to sound low and menacing with that cold still rattling around in her chest. "I'm asking *you*."

"Well, maybe I said something on the bus just now when all those kids were looking at me sideways and asking stupid questions. Maybe just to get rid of them I said that you knew I was telling the truth about my living in the past because you were born way back then too. That you'd already jumped over into the present ahead of me, but then, a couple of years ago, you ducked on back to 1850 to get me out . . ."

She was cracking her knuckles. It was a bad sign, and he gave her a sidelong look. ". . . because you'd left me behind when those slave trackers were shooting at me."

"Oh, terrific." Anna stopped under a street lamp just as it lit up above her. Although it was the middle of the day, clouds as dark as night were already rolling in. "What else did you tell the kids about me?"

"Look, Hanna—"

"My name is *Anna* here in the present. Got that? Anna

14

Post. Not Hanna Terwilliger. So I suppose you told them that my real mother and father ran a hotel in Indiana, and that there was a secret basement where your mother and my mother used to hide runaway slaves after they smuggled them over the river from Kentucky."

Rafe gazed into her eyes, and for a moment he seemed almost as old as she. "Tell me something. You're not proud of that?"

"Of course I am. But that's not the point. There's a reason why we all promised not to talk to anyone about who we really are and where we came from. People would think we were all crazy."

"So let them! I don't care!"

"Well, I do. And I don't thank you, Rafe Sims, for giving it away that I'm adopted."

"Anna, everybody in school knew that already. They've got older brothers and sisters who remember when you were first found and couldn't walk and didn't have any memory of who you were."

"Well, that's one thing. But you don't have to raise big questions about it so everybody can wonder if I'm so different from them."

"Then, a few years later, after summer vacation, you could suddenly walk, and now there was this black kid living in your house. You think they didn't talk about that? What's got into you that now you've got to be just like everybody else?"

"That's not true. But I don't have to let them know just how different I am."

"White girl, you *are* different! For one thing, you've got a black kid living with you. For another, you just name me

15

anybody else in that high school who ever crawled on her hands and knees into the past so she could save a runaway slave boy who was being shot at. Look, I didn't lie, did I? A dude is supposed to get in trouble when he lies, not when he tells the truth."

"While you were having this honesty fit," said Anna, coughing, "did you also mention the ghosts?"

Rafe paused while she tapped her soaking feet. "I don't think so."

"You better tell me exactly!"

"No, I didn't say anything, because I didn't ever meet your dumb old ghosts!"

Anna grabbed Rafe hard by the arm and whirled him around. "Those dumb old ghosts were my own real parents, and they are nobody's business but mine. So I want to be very sure about this. Look me in the eye, O Breaker of Promises. I don't want to hear one thing now and find out later you said another."

"Your ghosts," he flung back at her, "don't have anything to do with my dreams! So why should I have said anything about them?"

"*Dreams*? You're using dreams now for an excuse? What have they got to do with your blabbing?"

"Because my mother isn't in any of them, that's what they've got to do with it. Because first I forgot her voice, and now I can't even remember what she looked like! And even . . . and even if I do think I'm seeing her, it's when her back is to me and she's going off . . . and I chase after her but I can't catch up! So I thought that if I started to talk about her . . . to tell about her . . . and not hide anything anymore about me . . . then maybe . . . maybe she'd start comin' back in my—"

16

"Oh, Rafe, I'm so sorry."

She reached out to touch his arm, but he twisted away. Now he turned his back to her as well. She could see his shoulders quiver, and she knew he was choking down his sobs, hiding his tears.

Trying to ignore how cold she was getting, Anna reminded herself of how little time Rafe had ever actually spent with his mother. He'd been only a very small child when a white man he'd never seen before carried him away from his slave cabin while Rosalie, his mother, was working in the master's big house. The master's wife had sold Rafe to punish Rosalie for not paying enough attention to her own little boy while Rafe was sick. When Hanna Terwilliger's mother learned of this cruelty, she'd bought Rosalie and taken her out of the South to Indiana, then set her free. The two women became friends and spent the next five years looking for the boy—and setting other slaves free in the meantime.

While Anna was thinking this, Rafe must have been having similar thoughts. Now he said, "I didn't have her with me except for a few weeks after she found me again and busted me free! It wasn't even a whole month before the slave catchers looking for Mother Freedom caught up to us and shot her! And you want to know what's funny? I don't have any trouble at all remembering *their* voices and how happy they were they killed her! So listen, Hanna . . . Anna . . . whatever your name is—"

"Look, Rafe," she said gently. "It doesn't really matter when we're by ourselves. You can call me any—"

"I want to go back!" he shouted over her. "I want to get her body and bury it right. And then I want to go after those men and—"

17

"If you skipped back in time, Rafe, you'd only be seven years old again. There wouldn't be anything you could do."

"Never mind about that!"

"They'd just kill you. That's why we had to skip over."

"I'd find a way, I swear it. Maybe I'd even—"

"Look, Rafe, the thing to remember is that all your memories are still inside of you. I'm sure I can help you find them if you'd let me. In the beginning you couldn't get enough of my telling you stories about her. But then you wouldn't let me do it at all. You'd jump right down my throat if I started to speak about her. That was foolish."

"No, it wasn't! You had your own mother and father back then. You've got your memories of *them*. Plus you saw their ghosts, and I never saw mine! Why should you know *my* mother better than I do? That isn't fair!"

"I don't say it's fair. But that doesn't mean it's my fault."

"I'm not saying that it was your fault!" Rafe shouted. "First of all, Anna Post only lives in *this* world, with her boyfriends and her pajama parties and all that! As for Hanna Terwilliger, there was only one thing that was ever *her* fault. *She* knows what it is, but she doesn't want to *think* about it!"

Anna felt a sharp pang in her chest. "You think I should have skipped Rosalie over too?"

"Yes!"

She turned to face his glare. "But I couldn't."

"How do you know that?"

"Rafe, I tried to get her away. She died trying to save you!"

Rafe's eyes grew wide. He jumped back. "You're saying that I got my mother killed?"

18

"No!"

"Yes, you are!" he cried, backing away. "Thanks a lot, *Anna Post!*" Turning, he began to run.

She chased him most of the way around the long block. She would have caught him, too, if it hadn't been for her cold. Besides, he was in sneakers, and she was in slippers that squished on the wet pavement. When she realized that he was heading back toward the house, she slowed down.

It wasn't until she'd climbed the front steps that she saw him come out from the basement, pushing his bike. Anna started to run again, but Rafe was on the bike before she could catch up, jumping the curb and pedaling away.

TWO

Anna went into the house to make herself a cup of hot tea. She hated tea, but it was either that or start shivering. When Allan Post, her dad, came home at four-thirty from the library where he'd been working on his book, she told him what had happened. He hurried right back to his car and drove off to find Rafe. Barbara, her mom, came home from work an hour later, and Anna repeated the story. Barbara immediately got on the phone to call the minister of the Abyssinian Baptist Church where Rafe sometimes went to meet friends or think things over. The minister gave her several other numbers, and Mrs. Post called them too. But no one had seen Rafe.

As for Anna, she was in such a funk that she went upstairs and sank under her covers. Night came on while she read, did homework, watched TV. She even cried a little, but that didn't help either. Rafe didn't come home. The police were called, but they couldn't find him.

Lying in the dark, she began to wonder if Rafe wasn't right to blame her for failing to save his mother. Her thoughts went back to her last night as Hanna Terwilliger.

It had been her fault that Rafe had crawled off alone through the escape tunnel that led from the hideout beneath the Terwilligers' hotel. She'd let him go, then gone chasing after him, and had come out into the graveyard just in time to see the three men with long Kentucky rifles. They were slave trackers, hunting for Rosalie. Moving as silently as Indians in their deer-hide moccasins, they followed Rafe into the forest, letting him lead them toward the place where Mother Freedom was waiting for her boy.

But Hanna knew a more roundabout but quicker way to get there. Cutting away from them until she came to a meadow, Hanna bounded like a deer to another part of the creek. Her feet flew over the log bridge as she dashed madly toward the schoolteacher's cabin.

She spied the cabin in the darkness, a black lump under the trees. Something was stirring nearby. Out of the side of her eye she caught a glimpse of the runaway slave Rosalie had taken with her. The always-silent man was hidden away in the bushes with Papa's horse. Good, she thought, there was a chance for escape.

Hanna was at the rear of the cabin now. There was no window to call through, no time to get to the door. "Rosalie," she shouted through the back wall. "Get out of there quick. Them slavers are a-coming!"

Mother Freedom rushed outside, her pistol drawn. "Where's my Rafe?"

Hanna was panting hard, but still she heard loose stones falling. "He's down in the creek bed, a-tryin' to get here."

Rosalie cupped a hand to her mouth. "Rafe!" she boomed out. "Stay down there! Don't come up!"

Then that wonderfully brave woman rushed toward the creek, shooting at the men who were coming out from behind the trees on the other side.

The silent runaway cracked a twig loudly. Hanna turned, and he beckoned for her to come away with him. But she

21

wouldn't go. Not now. Not while she realized that she had lived through all this before . . . and done nothing! She'd done absolutely nothing but run away into another place and time, leaving both mother and son behind.

Rosalie, meanwhile, wasn't even taking aim as she ran toward the men, firing. She must have known that they were too far away for her pistol shots to hit them, but it did stop them from coming any closer to the deep slope of the creek into which Rafe had dashed.

That didn't trouble these men one bit, not while they had those sharpshooter rifles. When they took up positions and fired, Hanna saw Rosalie fall . . . saw her get up and shoot again.

Terrified, Hanna darted like the wind for the creek. Before the men could turn their rifles on her, she was already sliding feet first down the rocky bank.

Rafe had fallen, stunned by a rock that had come crashing down on his head. She tugged his arm and pulled him up. He was bleeding from a cut and didn't seem to know where he was or even who he was. But she made him stumble along beside her.

Behind her, Hanna heard men screaming for joy. "We got her! We got Mother Freedom! We get the reward!"

"String her up first. Then we'll take her back!"

"What are you talking 'bout? She's already deader'n a fence post."

"Hang her anyways!"

"Hold on, fellers. We're a-fergettin' 'bout the boy. Gonna make some reward money on him, too, ain't we? Lessen we want ter keep him private like fer ourselves, 'stead of returnin' him?"

"Figure that one out later! Let's git him! Where is he?"

"Beats me. I thought he went down here in the creek bed. Now I don't see hide nor hair of him. And that was a girl who just climbed down after him, wasn't it? 'Peared like the one we followed 'fore to that tunnel."

"Well now. We better hope we didn't shoot her up none. Nobody put up no reward for pluggin' no *white* folks. We could be arrested ourselves for that one, boys."

"I 'spect we got troubles then," said the man, sliding down the creek bank. "Look at this here rock. Got blood on it. Might be we shot her."

"You know what? We'd best finish both of 'em off and dump 'em somewhere. We won't say nothin' to nobody 'bout findin' that tunnel, just 'bout trackin' down the woman. That'd be the safest thing for us to do. Fan out, boys, and go down both sides of this creek till we get 'em."

But the children, hand in hand, were running . . . running . . . running. Hanna blinked. The creek bed was disappearing ahead of them into a great mist. "Rafe, faster!"

From behind came shouting. "I see 'em, boys! There they are. Shoot!"

The blood flowing down Rafe's forehead made it hard for him to see where he was going. Stumbling over a large rock, he tripped and fell to the side. Hanna fell with him just as rifle fire crackled overhead.

Then they were on their feet and running again.

The trackers were running too. There was another burst of gunfire as the children plunged into the mist.

And then they were in rain . . . hissing, drenching rain. Roaring noises came out of the darkness, and two great lamps came hurtling toward them at tremendous speed.

There was a loud warning blare. But Rafe, standing there wiping the streaming blood from his eyes, had no idea what was happening. Anna yanked him out of the way . . . and a huge eighteen-wheeler truck thundered by.

Anna looked around in amazement. They were in the middle of a highway with nighttime traffic roaring past in both directions. She had made it. She had gone back in time to fulfill her destiny and rescue Rafe as well as herself. The boy was no longer in that place between the living and the dead where she had left him the first time she had lived through all this.

At last these memories stopped playing before Anna like a movie on the ceiling. There was nothing else I could have done. Not a thing! she told herself, lifting her head from the pillow.

Meanwhile something—she knew not what—was drawing her attention toward the partly open window. The storm had grown worse. What was it that was so familiar about that dark mist outside . . . those sheets of drenching rain? Once again, Anna heard the distant sound of horns. Trucks . . .

"He's trying to go back!"

Caught up in her fears for Rafe's safety, Anna had no memory of her lightning-fast spring from the bed, or of dashing downstairs and seizing a raincoat to throw over her pajamas.

Kevin had been watching television in the living room until he'd heard Anna shout about Rafe's trying to go back. He made her tell him what was going on and stopped her from rushing out into the storm when all she had to do was phone for a cab. But the taxi service was too busy to send anyone to the house for another hour. As for her parents, they were still out, either cruising or down at the police station making out a missing-person report.

Now Kevin blocked the inside door to the basement, where the only remaining bike was kept. He wanted to go with her, he said. Better still, let him go after Rafe *instead* of her.

"You've already had your adventure!" he cried. "And you've got a cold!"

"What I've got is a brother who always butts in!" Shoving him aside, she practically tumbled down the steps to the basement, pulled out her bike, and pushed it up into the street.

How far did she have to pedal in this downpour to get there? Was it eight miles? Ten? "Don't think about it. Just do it one street at a time . . . and for God's sake, don't skid on the wet roads!"

Meanwhile, what was *Rafe* doing? Was he attempting to go back? And if he succeeded, wouldn't the slave hunters blow his brains out the first second he skipped over? Or would they carry him back to the squire to be beaten and starved for the runaway slave he was?

These thoughts made it possible for Anna to keep pushing herself harder and harder. But in the dark, the streets confused her. Swerving too quickly off a side road, she turned onto the wrong highway. The mistake made her angry with herself. She was losing time!

Anna's abrupt U-turn threw the bike into a skid. It jerked out from under her and sent her flying into the side of a pickup truck. If the vehicle hadn't been stopped for a light, it would have knocked her into the gutter, her legs under its rear wheels. Instead her chest slammed hard into the metal. The thud knocked the breath out of her and made her see stars before her eyes.

The driver felt the impact without seeing what had caused it. Thinking he'd been hit by some storm-crazed deer, he turned on his hazard lights and got out, swearing. There before him was a girl, looking half-unconscious, yet somehow clinging for dear life to the side of his vehicle. He stood in the road for a moment, scratching his head and waving other cars to go around him.

The man had to loosen Anna's arms before he could lead her by the arm to the passenger side of his truck. But she stopped at the door, saying dizzily, "My bike . . ."

The driver went to the shoulder of the road. Lifting the twisted frame, he tossed it into the back. "You can't ride it this way, kid. And I wouldn't let you anyhow. Get in. I'm taking you to the hospital."

"You don't have to. I'm all right."

"You positive?" He stared at her. "I don't want to feel like one of those hit-and-run guys."

"I'm sure. Really, I'm sure. I'm just shaken, that's all."

"Okay, good. You can show me where you live."

But it wasn't until they had both climbed inside the truck that Anna said, "I really appreciate this, but I'm not going home. If you could please take me somewhere else . . . it's not very far."

He gave her a long look. "Come on now. Don't tell me you picked a night like this to run away?"

"No, but somebody else did and I'm very worried, so I

have to find him. I have to do it right away!"

"You know, I think you're getting to be a problem . . ."

"I am. I know I am, and I'm sorry. But if you could just make a right turn and take me down that way. It's only about another five or six miles . . . I think."

"You *think?*"

"I'm almost sure."

"You know, I really wasn't going that way."

"You probably weren't going toward my house either," Anna declared, trying hard to manage a smile. She wanted it to be the kind that Mama had been so great at when she wanted to charm her way past the slave hunters almost one hundred fifty years ago. It was sort of a quivering, helpless little smile that Mama could put on when actually she was being as tough as a bobcat in a fight.

The driver frowned. "You're not trying to jerk me around, are you, kid?"

"No!"

"Good, because you're already trouble, and I don't want any more. I'll take you there, but I'm not hauling you back. Fair enough?"

"Yes! Thanks!"

The driver didn't say a word until Anna pointed to the shopping mall. Then he started to complain. "You must be kidding. This place is closed down. What is it—some druggie hangout? I can't just leave you here!"

"I'll be all right," she sang out, already hurrying across the parking lot into the stand of scrubby trees just behind it.

"What about your bike?" the man shouted. But there was no answer. Shaking his head, the man lifted her bike out of the truck and left it beside the road.

Anna could think of only one thing—that she might be too late. If only she had thought of this earlier, the moment Rafe had grabbed his bike. Rushing through the bushes, she stumbled over it.

She ran on, shouting his name. There was no answer. Ahead she saw the ditch. It was stuffed with junk, garbage, broken things.

Then sneakers . . . two overturned sneakers.

THREE

It was a long ride to the shopping mall. Rafe broke it up by pulling under the overhangs of different stores along the way to ask himself if he really wanted to go through with this. Any way he looked at it, the whole thing seemed dumb, dumb, dumb. It was probably the dumbest, most dangerous thing he could ever do. What was the sense of Anna ever having come to save him if he was going to skip back in time now?

A light switched on in his brain. There was the good reason for it! Maybe his mother really hadn't been killed back there by that slave tracker's shot. Maybe she'd only been wounded! Maybe he could rescue Mama out of the past before they could hang her. Yes! He'd use all his strength to lift her up, and he'd get her to the skipping-over place and bring her here to the present, where doctors could take care of her!

That was it, then. Rafe Sims was going to do for his mother what Hanna-Anna had done for him. And wouldn't everybody at home here be so glad to see him again!

Well, except for Kevin maybe . . . but probably him, too. The kid had just been feeling left out, that's all. It made Rafe laugh to think of Kevin calling what Rafe had been through an adventure. Some adventure, first to live as a slave, then to be hunted like an animal, and last to have your mother shot practically before your eyes.

He was going back. Back where he could see his mother's face again and hear that sweet voice sing.

Rafe was still thinking of her songs when the shut-down mall loomed ahead. The parking lot was broken and slippery under his wheels. He glided out to the back, got off, and left the bike in the bushes. Then he walked into the field beyond, pushing his way through the high weeds until he came to the remains of an old cabin. Now to find the exact place where he had first come into the 1990s, a weeping little boy of seven who thought he had lost his mother forever.

Where could it be? Down in that creek bed? It looked something like the one in Indiana where he and Hanna had been running for their lives in 1850. Or it would have, if not for all the broken bottles, blown-out tires, and other junk he could just barely make out in the blackness. Rafe climbed down into it, putting his hands out in front of him to break his fall in case he tripped.

One hand disappeared in front of his eyes. He jabbed the other arm farther out—and that one vanished up to the elbow.

Now he squatted down. Cautiously, ever so cautiously, he leaned into—

"There he be!" someone cried.

He saw a rifle being yanked up to firing level by a running man, saw the flash before he heard the shot. A burning whisper of death singed his ear, leaving the smell of gunpowder.

"Don't you move, little slave boy! Lessen you'd sooner be dead than go back to your master! Get him! Get him!"

All the trackers were moving toward Rafe now. He had

fallen forward on his face. He wanted desperately to scramble back, but he was too panicked to move.

Hands seized him by the ankles and tugged him hard. Rafe slid away as the men broke into a run and took aim to fire again.

The crash of sound was cut off when Anna fell on top of him. She lifted herself off and there was rain again.

Rain and the sounds of traffic.

And Anna in tears, crying, "You're bleeding! Your ear is bleeding."

The Posts, with Kevin in the lead, found them huddled together against the wall of the long-abandoned farmhouse behind the mall. While they were being rushed away through the downpour, Kevin's sharp eyes picked out Rafe's good bike and Anna's twisted one. These were somehow jammed into the trunk of the car, though it had to be left wide open to the rain.

Allan Post, sitting at the wheel, inspected Rafe's earlobe. Since it was bleeding freely, he figured there was no danger of infection. Barbara Post, sitting in the backseat, put her hand to Anna's forehead and shook her head, saying, "She's burning up."

As the car started to move, there was a quick conversation about what to do. Should they see if they could get hold of their doctor at this hour of the evening? Or should they drive straight to a hospital emergency room?

Anna, trying to keep her teeth from chattering, said, "We just want to go home, don't we, Rafe? We want to get into our own beds."

But Rafe, who was staring at nothing, barely nodded.

"He looks like he's in shock," declared Mrs. Post, biting her lip.

"No, I'm not," mumbled the boy in a low voice. "Hanna's right. I mean, Anna's right. Let's go . . . let's go home."

There was a question hanging in the air as they drove along. Finally Mr. Post asked it. "So, Rafe, you tried to go back to the past. What happened?"

Everyone waited so long for him to reply that they thought perhaps he hadn't heard them. "Not a thing," Rafe said firmly at last, shooting a warning look at Anna over his left shoulder.

He heard clucking coming from the seat just behind him. "You got a problem with that, Kev?"

"How did you get your ear cut if nothing happened?" the boy asked.

"Maybe I fell, man. Or maybe a dog did it. If I say nothing happened, that means *nothing*. What's it to you, anyway? You didn't live back then. That wasn't *your* mother!"

"Cool it, man."

Allan had said it gently, but Rafe made a face as he repeated, "*Cool it, man?* What are you trying to use black talk for? Most of the time you wouldn't get it right anyway. White people want everything. You even got to take our way of speaking from us!"

"Oh, Rafe," moaned Mrs. Post, heartsick.

The boy spun in his seat. "Hey, look! I don't need to live with you. What am I living with white people for?"

"Because we're your family now, you idiot!" Anna hissed at him.

"My family? Yeah, the whole world believes that one."

In a choked voice Mrs. Post asked, "Are things that bad

for you in school and out on the street?"

They all waited for an answer. "No," he said slowly, letting his voice drift away. "I don't have it bad at all, so don't worry 'bout that. I can take care of myself if I have to. I did so many a time back before my mama come to get me, so I can do it here too. But things are bad for other people. Lots of them. They ain't got no more hope than what I used to see on the plantation."

"Except now they can fight back!" said Kevin.

"Yeah . . . when they ain't fightin' each other."

"But, Rafe," cried Anna, "when you and I grow up, we'll do something to change all that."

"Uh-huh. You may be older'n me, girl, but you hardly know what you're talking 'bout. Seems like you've got to move mountains anytime you want to roll a peanut."

"Son, I may be out of line here," Mr. Post piped up gently, "but it appears to me that the way to honor your mother and what she was trying to do is to go forward, not into the past."

"Unless I belong there," Rafe said moodily.

They drove on in an uneasy silence until Mrs. Post took a stab at changing the atmosphere. "With all that's been going on, Allan, I suppose we can forget about the surprise."

She darted a hopeful look at the gloomy children, but only Kevin bit. "*What* surprise?"

She tapped his hand in gratitude and began to glow. "Well, your father got a letter from the sheriff who helped us look for Anna when she disappeared from the Ghost Hotel in Indiana."

"Honey, don't call it that."

"It was just a joke, Allan, to maybe lighten things up here."

"Some joke. The sheriff says it's been closed as a historical museum because kids from town are calling it just that. They've been daring each other to go down to the graveyard and disappear like Anna did. Then they get wild. They carry off things from the hotel or break them. They turn over stones in the graveyard. They—"

"Wait a minute," cried Anna, wide-eyed. "Are you talking about the headstones of my father and mother?"

A dazed and helpless look had replaced Mrs. Post's smile. "Maybe this wasn't such a good thing to bring up after all."

Rafe jumped in his seat. "See what I mean 'bout the way things is in this world? Look what stupid things people go and do."

Anna turned her frustration on him. "Rafe, will you please stop talking what you think is black talk!"

"Girl, I *am* black! That how we speak!"

"Bull! Black people speak all different ways like—"

"Like *real* people does, Anna-not-Hanna?"

"No, I didn't say that. Like everybody else do . . . does."

"Well, I don't wanna speak like everybody else! What you goin' do 'bout that?"

"Rafe can talk whatever way he wants," Mr. Post interjected dizzily. "And to finish what we've been trying to tell you . . . now that I've got my grant to keep working on my book, I thought it would be a good idea for us all to go down to the hotel during spring break to work on my research and fix up the place."

Rafe perked up. "You talking about research on Mother Freedom?"

"Certainly am."

"And what my parents . . ." Anna threw a hasty glance at Mrs. Post. "I mean, what the Terwilligers did to help runaway slaves too, right?"

"Of course!" exclaimed Mrs. Post. "And you don't have to call them the Terwilligers. They are your parents . . . too."

She was cut off by Rafe, who was suddenly excited and twisting in his seat. "Hanna! Do you think maybe my mother's ghost will turn up and look for me like your parents' ghosts came for you?"

"I don't know. I don't see why she wouldn't. Rosalie lived there too for a while."

"What I was trying to say," declared Mrs. Post, firmly taking back the conversation, "is that you don't have to talk about Colonel and Mrs. Terwilliger as if they are not . . . were not . . . your parents too. We've all been keeping the truth a secret from everybody else for so long that we've stopped living with it ourselves. But believe me, we have no objection to sharing you . . . and your love . . . with your memories of them. Right, Allan?"

"Right," said Mr. Post. "We consider it a great privilege to be raising the children of such heroes as your parents, Anna—and Mother Freedom, Rafe."

"I want to find out about my father too."

"He died before you were born," said Anna.

Rafe's face clouded over again. "How come you never told me that before?"

"Didn't your mother ever tell you?"

"No! You know she didn't!"

"Well, maybe it's because neither of us wanted you to feel any worse."

"Tell me now!"

"She said that he was beaten to death for trying to follow the Drinking Gourd north."

"Wait a minute. You saying my daddy was taking off and leaving my mother behind."

"She was pregnant, Rafe, and she couldn't do a lot of running or hiding. But the overseer was planning to murder him, so he had to go."

"That was no excuse!"

"Allan," snapped Mrs. Post, "I'm calling this trip off before it starts. These kids are obviously not interested in our surprise. And frankly I don't think I am ready to travel all the way down to Indiana with them in the car going at it like this. I wouldn't have the strength when I got there to help fix up that hotel."

Kevin stopped holding his ears, and Anna smiled brightly at her parents. But Rafe's eyes narrowed and his face set hard. So his mother had been left behind not once but twice. Well, he'd made a mistake trying to return to the past the way he had just attempted. That would only get him back too late to do anything but be shot down himself.

"Don't know 'bout the rest of you," he said, very low. "But I'm going."

It was one very rushed and busy week later that they all set out. Many hundreds of miles of driving lay ahead of them. When Barbara Post drove, they whizzed along on wide superhighways, making great time. But with Allan Post at the wheel it was another story.

Give him some falling-down hay barns and covered bridges to look at and he was in his glory, for he loved nothing more than reminders of "old-time America." His lovely detours along country roads took them hours out of their way.

"You know, in other families," declared Kevin, "the kids only ask: *When will we get there?* In ours it has to be: *How much farther are we now than when we started out?*"

"Patience, my dear ones," Allan said. "The goal is always less important than how you get there." And everyone groaned.

Everyone, that is, but Rafe, who stayed silent and inside of himself almost the whole way. Though seated by a window, he hardly glanced out of it. He napped whenever he could, asked no questions, and gave his answers in nods and shakes.

Everyone but Anna left him alone, even in the motels where they stopped at night. "Like it or not, you are still in this world," she whispered furiously while the rest of the family watched television. "So *be* with us."

But Rafe only nodded. After all the others were asleep, his eyes glittered in the darkness. He was thinking hard about his mother. Concentrating. He was trying to force himself to remember the face of Rosalie Sims. He listened for the sound of her voice as if he could summon her like a ghost from the dead.

FOUR

There was a hush in the car and all hearts beat faster. They were drawing closer to that large old house that once had held so many terrors and secrets.

"Hey, gang," chirped Allan, just to lighten things up. "The weather is a lot nicer than the night we first came here, when we couldn't see where we were going because of all that wind and rain."

"And Kevin was driving us all crazy," said Anna, "because he had to go to the bathroom."

"Hey!" cried her brother in annoyance.

"And then you, Anna," their mom put in quickly, "suddenly noticed during a lightning flash that there was a big building behind the trees. That seemed extremely odd to the rest of us, since nobody else had even *seen* a flash."

They sank back into their private thoughts. Anna recalled the morning after they had arrived at the old hotel. Just before dawn, she had wheeled herself into the lobby and found two old people in old-fashioned clothes. Although they looked at her strangely, they were very kind. As they questioned her about her life, they grew more and more excited. But it wasn't until the rays of the sun began to pass right through them that, with a great shock, she realized they were ghosts!

The couple claimed to be the spirits of her long-dead parents. They insisted that she too came from the past.

They said she had disappeared when she was nine years old. At first they had thought she'd been killed by the slave trackers who were trying to capture Mother Freedom. Then someone who was called the Conjure Woman had told them that their darling Hanna was still alive but had skipped over into another time. So here they were, waiting for her to finally be drawn back to the place of her birth, waiting to see her at last so their spirits could rest!

But Anna could not let it go at that. She'd followed the ghosts back to their graves, pleading with them to tell her more. She had always felt there was something she'd left undone, something that made her feel like a terrible coward and a deserter. Although she'd had no idea what that was, something had told her that unless she went back and fixed it, she'd never walk again.

From beneath the earth the ghosts had called to her to go down into her own tomb—the grave that had always been waiting for the missing Hanna. And she did.

Crawling around on her hands and knees, she found that the empty grave was the end of a long, narrow tunnel that led back to the house. Back to the past . . .

Anna was dwelling on all this as she sat in the rear of the car, between Rafe and Kevin. She looked at Rafe and suddenly knew what was on his mind.

From the way other faces were turning toward the boy, it seemed everyone else was thinking the same thing. "Son, forget that idea of making a dash of your own for the past," said Allan Post. "It just won't happen. Don't think that we don't know what really went on the last time you tried it. You very nearly got yourself killed."

Rafe didn't utter a word. He didn't have to. The smoky look in his eyes and his tightly clenched fists said it for him.

"There!" said Anna, pointing at the old wooden sign at the bottom of the dirt road that led up a winding path to the Terwilliger Hotel. But the nailed-up metal plate, which used to announce that this was a historical site open to the public, had been taken down. A thick chain was now stretched across the road.

"Some good it does keeping cars away," grunted Kevin, "when any kid who wants to come here can ride up on a bike."

Allan went up to a tree trunk and peered through his glasses. "Someone's carved a skull and crossbones into this tree trunk."

Kevin pointed farther up the path. "Yeah, and splashed red paint on that one!"

"They've trashed the place!" cried Anna. When Rafe mumbled something under his breath, she turned to him. "What?" she asked.

He mumbled something else, which could have been "Nothin'," and turned away.

"Rafe," Anna shouted, "what did you say?"

"I said," he shouted back, "what do you expect? That's what they do."

"Who do?"

"Whoever."

"Look, son," said Allan. "There is no slavery now. Anyone can go where they want and do what they want. Doesn't that count?"

"He doesn't want to think about that, Dad. He just wants to sulk about what still isn't right."

"Anna-not-Hanna, why don't you go soak your head," Rafe said. Then he whirled on Allan. "Sure it's better now. I don't say it's not better. But you go ask kids about slavery—even black kids—and they hardly know anything about it. And I'll tell you something—they don't even *care*. It's so hard to find anybody to care about anything except having money in their pockets. White or black, that's what they care about. Now some are gonna work at Burger King to get it. And some are gonna sell guns. And some are gonna push dope. And some are gonna to sneak into their old lady's purse. And some are gonna go through windows and rob. Do you think *money* was the big thing on Mother Freedom's mind?"

"I remember Rosalie talking a lot about it when she was saving up to buy your freedom," Anna said softly.

"That was for freedom! She was saving up for *freedom*!"

"People nowadays save for good things too, Rafe," suggested Barbara.

"Aw, you don't understand. Nobody understands. Just leave me alone."

The sound of flying pebbles interrupted them as a marked car pulled off to the shoulder of the road. "Hello again, Mr. and Mrs. Post," said the sheriff, lifting his tall body out of the vehicle and coming over to shake hands.

"Sorry if I kept you waiting. You're both looking much better than when I saw you last."

"Well, we certainly do feel better," declared Barbara.

The sheriff cocked an eye at Anna. "So this is the young lady who threw her wheelchair into the bushes and hitchhiked all the way up to New York State just to make a little craziness for her family and for law enforcement."

41

Anna stared at the ground while he hovered over her. She felt the pressure building as her parents waited for her to reply. They had warned her on the way down that she would have to deal with something like this. She had even rehearsed a nice apology for all the trouble she'd caused. But when the words came up to her mouth, they wouldn't go past her lips. Maybe it was because of that hard curl on Rafe's mouth and that *Girl, why-don't-you-just-tell-it-like-it-was?* look in his eyes.

"Oh, she was punished for that, believe me," Allan put in hastily when his wife gave him a little pinch.

"Grounded her for a whole week, did you?" said the sheriff, gazing at Anna as if she was the most spoiled princess in the world. "Maybe even took the private telephone extension out of her room."

"We did more than that," mumbled Allan.

"How much more?"

"Not a heck of a lot," he admitted. "We were just so relieved to find her again."

"But we did let her know how much pain and trouble she caused," declared Mrs. Post firmly. "And we still are extremely grateful for the way you and your officers comforted us and tried to help us find her."

The sheriff nodded. "Well, I'm glad it worked out. But I've been wanting to talk to this young lady for a long time, and now I'm going to. You'd been pretending to your folks all along that you couldn't walk, hadn't you?"

"No."

"No? You expect me to believe that the morning after you came here a miracle happened?"

"She wasn't lying to us, Sheriff," interrupted Barbara

hastily. "Anna really was not able to walk then. But the reason for it lay in her mind. And—"

"I saw the ghosts," Anna blurted.

"Oh, you did?" said the sheriff. "Then what?"

Anna longed to tell the whole truth, but Mom was miserably biting her lip and Dad was sending desperate glances her way.

How could Anna get herself out of what she'd started? "The ghosts convinced me I could walk," she said. "And I did."

The sheriff rubbed his jaw. "Which made you so happy that you ran away from your folks?"

Anna dropped her eyes. "No . . . well . . . yes. Something like that. Actually, I just wanted to show them that I could take—"

"Never mind. I don't want to hear more lies. Let your family put up with that. I won't."

As Anna flushed beet red, he pointed a finger. "But I am going to say this just once. If there are any more *miracles* around here, I guarantee that this time you are going to find out what a lot of trouble is really like."

Mr. Post stepped in quickly to put his arm around Anna's shoulder. "Sheriff, that was a wholly unnecessary warning."

"I sure hope so, because I am tired of dealing with the mess that her last disappearance made for us, once the news of it got out. We had a kid who tried crawling into that escape tunnel and most of it fell in on him. Luckily his friends got him out before he suffocated, but he was still unconscious when they got him to the hospital."

"That's terrible!" cried Anna.

"Glad you think so."

43

"And I am sorry for what I—"

Her remark brought an angry snort from Rafe.

The sheriff jabbed a finger in his direction. "Who's this?"

"Me? I'm the runaway slave she brought back from the year—when was it, Hanna?—1850, and I am the son of Mother Freedom!"

"Oh boy!" The sheriff was still shaking his head as he walked to the big padlock on the chain across the driveway. "I'm beginning to wonder if it was such a good idea to let you folks up there at all."

"They'll behave!" said Barbara. "I promise you they will."

"I hope so," he declared, unlocking it while everyone got back into the car. "I certainly hope so."

"Look at this! This is a disgrace," Mr. Post said when he saw all the crushed soda and beer cans and all the other trash lying in the road.

"So we'll clean it," cried his wife. "Calm down. This is why we brought all the garbage bags."

"But this place is a part of our history."

"Ha!" sniffed Rafe. "Like anybody out there cares about history."

Mr. Post turned on him, fuming. "How long are you going to be negative? You have been putting down everything on this trip. If you can't say a word even halfway friendly or gentle or constructive, then why don't you say nothing at all?"

Rafe crossed his arms as if he didn't care, but Anna knew better. "Dad, do you think *you've* been friendly or gentle or constructive?"

"No . . . I suppose not." He sighed. "I'm sorry for coming

down on you so hard, Rafe. Let's both forgive and forget. Okay?"

There was no answer.

"Could you give me some response, son?"

"Don't call me son. I ain't your son."

"I give up!" Mr. Post gave the wheel a last turn before the car rolled into an open meadow.

Kevin ran ahead as everyone got out of the car. He came back, saying, "There's a lot of windows smashed. They've been lobbing rocks at them. And I think there are some BB holes too."

"Great," sighed Mr. Post. "Well, let's go inside and see it all."

The porch itself was in decent shape, but the glass doors to the lobby were also smashed. Anna dreaded what she would find inside—and with good reason. The wicker furniture was overturned, some of it broken, some of it charred with cigarette burns. There were initials carved into the hotel's mahogany desk, and its bell was missing. The brass spittoons were black inside as if fires had been set in them.

Mrs. Post's arm went around Anna's waist. "We'll fix it up, darling. You'd be amazed at how things can be restored to look as they used to. Isn't that right, Allan?"

"I don't know what's been done to the rest of the place," her husband replied. "But just from what I see here, it's going to cost more than we expected."

His wife threw him a hot look. "So we'll get donations! Right, Allan?"

He glanced at Anna, shuffled his feet, and nodded. "Right," he said, with a comforting smile. Then he set off for the guest rooms down a hall.

"Not too bad," he called back with a sigh of relief. "We'll do what we can while we're here this week, then make a list of the rest and come back in the summer. Let's get our stuff and pick out our rooms."

"Anna-not-Hanna—"

"Stop calling me that, Rafe!"

"Okay. Show me again how I get to the hiding place."

"Follow me!" cried Kevin, dashing past them excitedly. "I'm the one who found it when Anna was missing!" Throwing open a door to a short corridor, he ran past the rooms on both sides, calling, "Then you go down to the last one. That was Hanna's!"

But Anna, with a pang in her heart, stopped outside the room in which Amos and Dora Terwilliger had slept so many years ago. Her hand hesitated on the knob. What if everything inside had been wrecked too? She opened the door slowly, eyes half closed . . .

But there was her sweet mother's dressing table and her father's clay pipe in its rack. She took it out, brought the bowl to her nose. It still had the smell of his tobacco! She lingered over other objects in the room, touching them . . .

Then she heard scraping, shoving noises. "Careful!" she warned, rushing to her own bedroom. Toys, playthings, her bed, and her old crib were still there—nothing broken. The boys were moving her dresser to lift up the woven rug covering the wooden trapdoor.

Rafe yanked it open. The three of them peered down the steep ladder to the stone floor of the musty little room. This was the secret room where, for three weeks, a runaway slave boy, like others before him, had once lived.

Rafe didn't want anyone else to go down with him now.

He asked them to leave him there for a while. He didn't come out until hours later, after there had been a cleanup on the lawn and Barbara came to ask him if he wasn't starving like the rest of them. They were all thinking of going to town for pizza.

"That's okay," he said.

"If that's what you want . . . but, darling, it's cold and dark down there. Pretty soon you won't get any light from up here."

"Can I have a flashlight from the car? And my sleeping bag, too?"

"You're not planning to spend the whole night down there, are you?"

"Yes, I am."

"But why?"

"'Cause if my mother's ghost is coming to find me, she won't do it in that lobby like Hanna's folks did. She'll do it right here, where I always was."

"Oh, Rafe, I do hope she comes! You deserve it so. Still . . . you won't be afraid?"

"Afraid?" he snorted. "Of my own mother?"

"That would be foolish, I suppose, wouldn't it?"

"Certainly would."

Barbara hung there, biting her lip again. "But you just can't count on . . . on her showing, you know."

"If she can do it," said Rafe with determination, "then she will. And she can, 'cause my mama could do anything anybody else could do!"

"Yes. Yes, I believe that."

"Oh, and when you come back, could you bring me an orange soda and a couple of slices with sausage?"

Mrs. Post cheered up at once. "Of course, baby. We'll be back in a little bit with your food."

For the rest of that day and most of the night, Rafe lay in the darkness waiting for Rosalie Sims. It was while he lay in a doze that he felt something like a breath of air on his face. His eyelids flew open.

She was hovering over him, looking thin, shriveled, older than he had ever seen her.

"Mama?" Rafe whispered, like the little boy he had once been.

"No, chile, no," said the low and crackling voice. "When I was alive, they call me the Conjure Woman."

A chill ran through him, and he sat up straight.

"I don' mean you any harm, chile. I was a good frien' to yo' mama in life. I gave her the tea that fix her heart when she was sick. Was a frien' to Hanna's mama too, when her little girl didn't come back. That woman like to go out of her mind till I tole her that the chile had skipped over to where she be out of harm's way. So what you come looking for, chile? You wants to be with yo' mama?"

He nodded. The old woman stretched her long bony hand toward him.

"Has you come to be wit' her in death? Touch my hand, chile."

Rafe felt the hair rising on his head, and he jumped back, crying. "No, no, not to be dead. I want to go back to before she was killed. I want to change things."

"Supposin' you cain't change things?"

"I don't believe that. I *won't* believe it! But if not . . . then I want to be with her anyway. Please tell me where she is. Why didn't she come to me?"

"Come to you how? Like I is now, a ghost? Mother Freedom, she don't hold with that. She always did believe the dead should stay quiet, lessen they scare the livin'. But I was always so used to conjurin' up ghosts that I don't think that way. When I hears you calling for yo' mama, I done took pity on you."

"Didn't she hear me too?"

"She don't want to hear. And she don't want you to come back to when she was alive, so she have to do the same thing all over. She know you done skip over to freedom, and she want to leave it that way."

"But I'm not free!" He jumped to his feet. "You tell her I'm not free. And I'll just turn real bad unless I go back and help her!"

The ghost was starting to fade. "I'll say one thing 'bout you, Li'l Rafe, then I'm gone."

"What?"

"When it come to wantin' what you want, you jest like your mama."

Rafe didn't think that was a bad thing. In fact, the ghost left him feeling pretty good about himself . . . and more determined than ever. Now he knew for certain what he was going to do.

The next morning he was the most cheerful person at cleanup. All the work so far had been inside the hotel and on the grounds just outside. Now he said to Anna, "Let's go down to the graveyard and see if the tombstones are all right."

So far, Anna had been avoiding that. It wasn't that she didn't want to visit her mother's and father's graves. She was afraid of finding their stones knocked down or smashed.

But the only damage she and Rafe found was at the site of her own empty burial place. Even there, the stone was still standing. Once again, Anna read the chiseled words:

THIS GRAVE LIES WAITING FOR OUR DEARLY BELOVED CHILD, HANNA. BORN 1841. DIED 1850. BY SLAVE HUNTERS SOMEWHERE CRUELLY MURDERED.

The grave itself—and the mouth of the escape tunnel that had long ago been built into it—were crushed down as if by a bulldozer.

"Well, that's not so bad." Anna sighed and began stuffing trash into the large plastic bag she had taken with her.

As Rafe helped her, she looked up and said, "You've been just awful to everyone lately, you know that?"

"Sure."

"You do know that this family loves you, don't you?"

Rafe nodded. "I love them too."

"Yet you treat us so badly sometimes."

"You don't have to tell me. I just can't help it."

"But why?"

"I don't know." He shrugged. "Maybe it's because there are times when I feel bad about leaving my mother back there."

"Rafe, she wanted you to escape."

"You just don't see, Hanna. That's why it's my fault. If it hadn't been for me, she would have gotten away."

"Do you really think she'd want you to punish yourself because she gave her life for her son?"

"Maybe it won't have to be that way this time when I go back."

"Go back? Rafe, look what happened last time you tried! You were almost—"

50

"That was the wrong way to do it. I've got to go back just the way you did it. I have to go through the tunnel to *before* she got killed."

"But, Rafe, I could only skip *you* over, not her. The ghosts told me that your spirit couldn't be found among the dead. It was stuck somewhere, so it was possible to bring you forward. Your mother's already gone forever."

"Maybe, maybe not. But I've got to do something! Don't you see that? Can't you just tell me you're on my side whatever I do?"

"I'm always on your side, Rafe. But this tunnel collapsed! It fell in on someone, who nearly got killed."

"Sure, *this* end. But the other end is open in the hidden room. That's why they put an iron grate with a lock on there to cover it. Did you hear a bang last night?"

Anna stared at him.

"Answer me."

"We did hear a noise. Kevin thought some kids had set off a firecracker."

"That was me, when I blew that lock right off with this." Rafe reached under his shirt and drew a pistol from his belt.

Anne was stunned. "Where did you get that!"

"From the big brother of a friend of mine. I traded him for it the day after they clipped my ear. This time I'm gonna blow those trackers away before they even have a chance to shoot at my mother! I won't feel bad about it, either. If I put them away first, my mother will be able to live a whole life and do what she has to do, like Moses did, to set our people free."

Anna was wild-eyed. "Rafe, you can't take something like that back into the past!"

"Why not? My mother had a pistol too, and she used it."

"But this one is not from that time. You just can't."

"We'll find out about that."

"I'm telling you, Rafe, if you go back, you'll only be seven years old again. Those men knew what they were doing. I couldn't fool them when I tried to; that's how they learned where the escape tunnel was. They were trackers and they moved without making a sound. If you had that gun and you tried using it on them, they'd kill you for sure. I'm telling you, I'll stop you from going if you don't give it to me."

"You want it? Here!" Rafe heaved the pistol into the woods. "But you have to help me now! I need to clear out the front of this tunnel. This morning I started by myself, but it's going too slow. If you love me, Anna-not-Hanna, you're going to do it!"

"Rafe, that's the kind of work that took Papa weeks!"

"I don't have weeks. That's why I need you. Kevin too, since he always feels left out."

"You heard the sheriff warn us all about making more trouble for him."

"Just don't tell him I'm gone. Then there won't be any trouble."

"You can't ask for that!" Anna cried, turning away. "You just can't!"

He watched her run madly up the hill. "Girl, don't you dare tell on me!" he called after her. "Promise!"

She didn't answer, and in another moment she was gone. Rafe stayed in the graveyard, looking at the stones.

He felt like crying. "If I knew you were buried here, Mama, where I could put flowers on your grave. Even if I could just remember your face . . . your voice . . ."

He didn't notice that Anna had turned back, nor did he hear her coming down the hill. "All right, but I'll go with you," she murmured, slipping her hand into his.

"That's really good," he said softly.

"So will I," boomed Kevin, emerging from his hiding place among the trees. "This time *nobody's* leaving me out!"

FIVE

There were four nights of secret digging at the cemetery. The children spent half of the first one using Allan's car jack to pry out the big rock the police had jammed into the tunnel's entrance. Then they hunted among the trees for pieces of wood to push up the tunnel ceiling while the actual digging went on.

There was only one rusty old shovel. Rafe insisted on being the one to crawl ahead and use it. The others worked just behind him, putting up the walls and taking the buckets full of dirt that he passed through his legs like a football player hiking a ball.

"Rafe, watch what you're doing!" Anna said to him more than once when he knocked against the roof of the narrow little tunnel. "There's almost as much dirt falling down on you as you're digging. You're getting too tired to be careful. Come on out. It's my turn, then Kevin's."

"Don't worry about me," Rafe told her after she backed up to let him come out at last. "Nothing's gonna happen to the spark of justice!"

"What is this spark of justice stuff?" Kevin asked as he came back to the open grave from dumping a bucketful of dirt in the woods.

"That's what a pastor in the Underground Railroad told Rosalie she was the night we smuggled Li'l Rafe over into Indiana," Anna explained.

"So, bad things don't happen to sparks of justice?"

"They sure do," said Anna. "That's why this ten-year-old spark is going to sit down somewhere and rest before he blows out."

So it went, until Allan Post got up in the middle of the night to go to the bathroom and his flashlight wouldn't turn on. This was a bit strange, he thought, since he'd just changed the batteries the day before. "Maybe I put them in the wrong way," he muttered to himself, unscrewing the back.

He woke his wife to inform her that the batteries were gone. "Can't this great mystery wait until tomorrow?" she muttered into her pillow.

"I suppose. But if this is a trick, it's a very strange one. The kids have a working flashlight for themselves, so why . . ."

She sat up slowly. "Maybe we should be asking ourselves something else, Allan. Like why is it that they all look so worn out in the morning?"

"That part hasn't bothered me. Kids will keep each other up on vacation."

"I wouldn't call this a vacation, by any means. Look where we are. And then there are those funny glances they keep throwing our way when they don't think we're looking."

"Well, I guess I really haven't noticed. What do you mean by funny?"

"It's as if they're watching to see if we're watching *them*. Or as if they feel guilty about something. I'm not sure. But now I *am* getting worried."

"Well, should we wait till tomorrow to ask them what's going on? Should we spy on them? Or should we do a combination of both? First we can show some faith by asking. Then, after they lie to us, we can feel we have every right to snoop."

"It's not a joke, Allan. Don't forget what happened the last time we were here."

"You're thinking about Rafe?"

"Yes."

"Let's go."

Barefoot, they padded into a hall that would have been pitch-black if it hadn't been for the moonlight coming in through the broken-glass entrance from the porch. Barbara gave her husband's arm a tight squeeze as they approached the lobby.

"Don't worry," he whispered. "They aren't *your* ghosts. Besides, Anna never sees them now. Didn't she tell us they're at rest since they'd already found her?"

"Yes, but I'm not afraid of them. In fact, I'd *like* to see them. I want to tell them how wonderful she is, and what she means to *us*. And I want to ask them not to take her back there again—not for any reason!"

"What's that?" He nodded at a dim bit of fog near the broken door in the lobby.

"Take it easy, Allan. It's just a bit of mist that's drifted in, that's all."

"How is it then that we don't see any mist *outside?* Look what's happening to it now."

The thin wisp of fog had begun to take on a shape. "Anyone there?" Barbara asked, squeezing Allan's arm.

"Oh yeah," a quiet voice replied. "Someone."

"Hanna's mother?"

"No, she won't be coming back. Once I was called the Conjure Woman."

"Why, yes," said Barbara shakily. "My daughter has mentioned you. You were the one who—"

"Not now, please." The Conjure Woman lifted a ghostly cane. "I wants to ask you to do something fo' Rafe."

"Do? Do what?"

"Don't make it no harder on him to go."

Allan glanced sharply at his wife, then at the ghost. " Go where?" His voice rose to a shout. "Do you mean that rotten tunnel? Have they been digging it out? Is that what they're doing?"

"What is it with you ghosts?" screamed Barbara. "Is it because you're not alive that you have to play with the lives of others? Don't you dare toy with the lives of children!"

"Barbara, come on!" To the ghost, Allan cried, "I don't know if you mean well or ill. But we have to use our own judgment!"

"Be sure it's a good one then," whispered the voice as the ghostly form dissolved into emptiness.

Allan and Barbara barely heard her. They burst out of the hotel, shouting as they ran. "Rafe! Stop! Please, Rafe! Wait till we get there. Anna! Kevin! Don't you dare help him!"

Rafe was already standing in the shallow grave when he heard their cries. "You tell them I always loved them, even when I was a pest," he said quickly. "Got to get going now."

"This is marvelous," murmured Anna, blurry-eyed with tears. "I'm losing you forever and being yelled at at the same time."

"Don't say things like that now. It makes me feel terrible about going. If I can bring her back, I will, just like you did with me."

"But that tunnel isn't as strong as it used to be. Any little thing will make it all fall in."

The Posts were already in sight. "Anna-not-Hanna, you know I have to do it! Kevin, shake my hand."

"Forget that, because I'm going too! You can't stop me. I'm smaller than you, and I can fit through it better."

"Yeah, and what are you gonna do if you get there?"

"That's easy," said Kevin, brightening. "I'll have an adventure. You know, like Huckleberry Finn!"

"Forget it. It's too dangerous!" said Rafe, curling down like a cat to put his head into the tunnel's mouth. "Anna, you'd better not let him do anything dumb." He squeezed his head and shoulders through. Then he was gone.

"If I want to do something dumb, I will!" cried Kevin, jumping into the grave after him and going down on all fours.

"No, you won't!" Throwing herself to the ground, Anna reached down to make a grab for his legs. He was too quick for her to get hold of anything but his ankles. She pulled with all her might—and hardly budged him. From inside the tunnel came muffled screams and curses. Clawing the ground and wedging himself against the sides of the tunnel, Kevin was fighting back.

When their parents ran up to Anna, she was still on her belly over the open grave, frantically tugging. Mr. Post went down beside her. "Let me!"

"I can't, Dad!" she cried. "If I let go, he'll get away."

"I've got him," Allan panted. "Give me room." But the instant that Anna released her brother's feet, Kevin gave a terrific yank, broke free of Allan's hands, and disappeared completely into the tunnel.

Barbara's "Out of my way!" had barely left her mouth before she slid headfirst all the way down into the grave. Her long, thin arms shot into the tunnel's mouth, but her searching fingers could not touch him. "Kevin!" she cried. "Kevin! Rafe! Oh, God, we're losing them. Allan, do something!"

"Do what, Barbara? What?" He paused. Suddenly he made a dash for the hill. "I'll go to the other end, where the old hidden room is!"

"Mom, Rafe has the right to try going back. But if you come out of there and let me by, I'll go after Kevin," Anna offered.

"No, you won't. I won't let you go in there again." Mrs. Post spread her arms over the grave, blocking the way down.

Meanwhile, Allan Post ran up the hill, the steps, and across the porch. Gasping, he flung himself through the lobby, then behind the desk and into the old Terwilliger apartment, where he stumbled to the trapdoor. He lost his footing on the steep ladder. The three rungs he missed bumped his face as he slid down.

None of this even took his attention now. In the soft light of dawn coming down from the trapdoor in Hanna Terwilliger's little bedroom, he made out the wider end of the tunnel. Stepping over scattered mounds of rubble the children had yet to smuggle out of the house, he began calling to the boys.

At last he heard a distant voice crying, "Slow down! Wait up. Wait for me . . ."

Allan gave a prayer of thanks as he made out a huddled form coming toward him in the darkness. "You're almost there!"

"*Dad?*"

"Yes, Kevin. Keep coming."

But the crawling boy stopped dead in his tracks. "Then this isn't the *past?*"

"It's not the past, Kevin. Come on out."

Dark suspicion trembled in the next question. "Where is Rafe?"

"I don't know. I haven't seen him yet."

"He left me behind! It isn't fair!"

"What are you doing, Kevin? Why are you backing up? Don't turn around!"

But Kevin scurried deeply into the tunnel once more, his hands and his hopes searching together for a secret passage into an adventure that belonged to someone else.

SIX

When Li'l Rafe came out of the crawl tunnel on his hands and knees, he was feeling so strange that he grew dizzy when he tried to stand up in the hiding place. To keep from falling, he had to press against the rocky wall. There he waited, blinking hard until the chair and the tiny writing desk and the sleeping mat on the stone floor all stopped spinning.

But here was something that didn't make sense. The lamp Mrs. Terwilliger had filled up and lit for him after bringing him his supper was flickering low. Rafe didn't think he'd been in the tunnel *that* long. He'd only crawled down to the end of it for a peek into the graveyard, then turned right around to come back again. Now that didn't take no kind of time at all—even if you did count a-getting all dreamy on the way back.

And why was he feeling so hungry, like he hadn't eaten in hours and months and years? He glanced up at the little air hole in the ceiling, but hardly any light ever came through there anyway. Well, if a long time really had gone by, then Mama would be back soon. She'd come down here and tell him stories and talk to him—and he'd know she was safe.

If only there was something to do in here! Used to be he and Hanna would spend the whole day together. Either she was a-helping Mrs. Terwilliger learn him reading and writing or he was showing her all the good songs he knew.

Then they'd play at things like shootin' marbles on the stone floor or even upstairs on her rug. Well, he could do all that practicin' and singin' and shootin' right now if he wanted to. Only he just didn't feel like it no more.

Hanna. She was off with Mother Freedom tonight, both of them giddyupping in that buggy to all the different places where runaways might have ducked into after they crossed the Ohio River to the freedom side here in Indiana.

Some freedom side, with him having to hide down in this hole till he didn't hardly know what the sunshine felt like no more. Sometimes he thought this was what it felt like to be dead. Leastways when he was alone like this. It wasn't right at all, his Mama goin' everywhere with Hanna. *He* was Mother Freedom's one and only *real* child, not her!

Rafe knew, of course, that nobody was at fault here. There were reasons why a dressed-up white girl should be sitting in front when a black woman went a-bouncin' along through the town and up some country road in a fancy buggy. That made it look as if Hanna was being brought home from a party or had been visiting somebody. Nobody would wonder what Rosalie Sims was really doing so close to the river where boats were going up and down with slave catchers in them ready to shoot to kill.

That hungry feeling was like a punch in the stomach. His eye drifted to the tiny desk that had once been Hanna's. He didn't expect to find anything in the drawer, but he yanked it open anyway, then shut it just as quickly. There wasn't even a biscuit inside—not even a crumb! Why couldn't they put a sandwich in there for him? He should have stayed in that graveyard and gone looking among the bushes for berries. That place didn't scare him one single bit. If he met a ghost there, it wouldn't bother him at all. Still, it did make the top of his head tingle when, on the way back, it seemed like there was a boy calling after him: *Wait, Rafe, wait. Wait for me.* . . .

A spooky feeling came over Rafe like a wave as he thought about this. Suppose he *had* seen a ghost, and it had followed him all the way through the tunnel. Suppose it was in this room with him *right now* . . . there in the corner maybe, where the flickering light didn't go. It was the ghost of a pesky little white boy who didn't want to stay where he belonged and kept jabbering about how he was being "left out." There seemed to be a man there too, telling the boy not to cry and saying that Rafe had to leave his other life behind, that Rafe had a special thing to do just like . . . like Anna? . . . like Hanna had—that he had to save his mother!

Rafe was shaking now. Was this some kind of wide-awake *dream*? Mama had said there was all kinds of foretellin' truth in dreams if somebody knew how to read 'em like the Conjure Woman did.

Maybe all this dreamin' was just his stomach trying to make him think 'bout something else. If only he had just one big cookie from Hanna's cookie box.

Rafe blinked hard. That box was so clear in his mind, like it was just waitin' for him to come and get it. His gaze traveled up the ladder to the trapdoor in the ceiling. There never had been anything in the whole world that tasted like the cookies Mrs. Terwilliger's aunt Ida had sent all the way from her plantation.

The little rug in Hanna's room slid to one side as the flat slab of wood in the floor rose up on its hinge. Swiftly and silently, Rafe came out and hurried to the dresser. But the round tin box was gone.

Girl done took it with her! he thought. Now isn't that somethin', when she can just go down the hall and into the hotel kitchen anytime she wants!

Well, maybe there was something good to eat in Mama's room, like one of those chocolates she was fixing to give to the Conjure Woman, who was healing her with roots and teas.

Rafe put his ear to the crack at the door. There wasn't a sound in the corridor. Like a shadow, he flitted across it and into his mother's room.

It had been days since the Terwilligers had let him go in there and lie down beside her while she was getting well. Just being there now gave him such a good feeling that his stomach didn't pain him so hard now. Besides, taking from Mama without her knowing it felt like stealing.

Rafe turned to go. He was just heading for the door when he heard a soft noise in the corridor. Was it a foot coming down very carefully? Was someone sneaking around out there? He thought of Hanna's room where he had left the trapdoor to the hidden room wide open for anyone to see. Now that it was too late, he suddenly was paying attention to all Mama's warnings about hired snoops for the slavers. She'd said there were men who might come into the hotel pretending to be guests on vacation, when they were really hunting for evidence to destroy the Underground Railroad and everyone connected with it!

Now the knob began to turn. The door was cracking open.

"Hold!" barked a voice that rang out down the corridor like a whip. "Move away from that door!"

The hand that held it moved away, and the man to whom it belonged said, "Goodness me, sir. Is there a problem? You seem all in a dither, if I may say so."

"You may say what you are doing here. This part of my hotel is private. You do not belong here."

"Bless my soul. Did I get turned around by mistake? I suppose I came out of the wrong door of the dining room, and I—"

"From there you had to go through two other doors to get here. One of them was clearly labeled *Owner's Apartment*."

"My regrets then. But my spectacles were in my pocket and there were thoughts on my mind. I assure you that I did not have any intention of—"

"Of what, sir? Of lurking by the door before you started to open it?"

"This is most offensive, sir. I tell you, I mistook this for my room. I am a man of honor and I do not *lurk*. And you have no right to speak in such a rude manner to a paying guest in this hotel."

"I've had my eye on you for days, and I do not believe you. Nor do I want your money. You are no longer welcome at this hotel. Kindly leave."

The intruder's voice grew hard. "I have challenged men to pistols at dawn for less, Terwilliger. Apologize for your tone."

"You may call me *Colonel* Terwilliger. That was my rank when I left the army after the Mexican War. If you long for a duel to the death, feel free to demand one."

There was a pause. "That time may come soon enough. But right now, business before pleasure."

"Then quickly state your business."

"I am an investigator for the Southland Property Owners Association down in Louisville. We recover missing property for our clients."

"You mean runaway slaves."

"Just so. But my particular interest at the moment is closing down stations along the Underground Railroad and seeing to it that the criminals who operate them are sent to prison."

"That has nothing to do with me."

"Does it not?"

"Have you any proof that it has?"

"Well, I know that you have working for you a certain Rosalie Sims, who we strongly suspect goes secretly by the name of Mother Freedom."

"I have never heard of any Mother Freedom. Suspicions are not evidence. What's more, Mrs. Sims . . . Rosalie . . . is no runaway. My wife bought her several years ago, then set her free. We have the bill of sale to prove it."

"Free or not, she's committed violence in order to steal from his rightful owner a boy named Little Rafe. There is a warrant for Sims's arrest in Kentucky. Once she faces justice down home, I'm sure we'll have no problem proving what else she's done. There is already a price on this so-called Mother Freedom's head. The woman will hang for her crimes. Captain, where is the boy?"

"I have no idea. But she paid good money to buy that child's freedom. I personally sent it for her, and I can prove it."

"The sale never went through."

"The squire and his lawyer certainly did not return the money. The lad has a legal right to his freedom."

"That will be decided when we bring Little Rafe back with his mother."

"So you were going through these rooms to look for him?"

"As a matter of fact, yes, I was. And if you had any sense—"

"Whether or not I have any sense is beside the point."

"I think he's on the other side of this door right now. I know for a fact there is someone in there listening."

"You're moving that shoulder too close to the door," said Hanna's father darkly.

"No matter. I can get a sheriff or a marshal to come with a search warrant."

"Then why haven't you?"

"Oh, some of these northern judges are stalling because they don't like the new law that the U.S. Congress just passed for recovering fugitives. It will just take another day or so of twisting arms to get a warrant signed. I was merely being impatient."

"I'm afraid you will have to be impatient somewhere else."

"Unhand me, sir! I will leave on my own!"

"That is acceptable to me. Get your things at once."

Rafe was terrified. Even now he trembled, though it was more in fear for his mother than himself. The slavers were closing in on her. If she didn't stop her work, somebody was going to kill her. He recalled Hanna's mother saying just the other day, "Rosalie, everybody seems to know who you really are. Just as soon as you're ready to make the trip, I want you to take your son and head north. I'll help you memorize the line of stops to Rochester and the address of

Mr. and Mrs. Post. They'll get you over into Canada. Promise me you'll go."

Oh, how he had wanted to hear her say she would. But no. Sick as she'd been, she sat right up, saying, "You don't listen, Dora. I tells you I got work to do. You knows very well there's black people in hidin' all over now." He'd watched his mother get to her feet, swaying like a tree top in a high wind.

"But just look at you!" Mrs. Terwilliger had said. "You're in no condition to do anything yet. I am the one who's going looking tonight instead of you."

"Oh, Dora, you means well, but you talkin' nonsense. Most of them runaways won't trust no white woman who comes sneakin' around to find them. But I knows a hundred places they likely to be duckin' in at."

All at once Rafe understood why he'd been daydreaming about saving his mother's life. She wasn't goin' to do it for herself, that's why! It was up to him to find a way. And he would!

My mama, he told himself, went down into slavery land like Moses into Egypt till she fetched me out. I ain't goin' let nothin' happen to her.

This wasn't some ordinary cross-his-heart-and-hope-to-die kind of vow. He needed a way to make it too holy to ever be broken, no matter what. Casting about, he snatched up her pillow, planted kisses on both sides, and put it back. There! Better go now and get to the ladder and find some way to slide Hanna's rug back over the hatch as he went down. Tiptoeing to the door, pausing to listen for any noise in the hall, Rafe began to turn the knob.

But something held him back. Something about the feel

of her pillow against his face a moment before was making him look back at that narrow brass bed. There wouldn't do any harm if he only stayed for a minute.

Rafe made a little hill of the blanket until it felt something like his mama lying right up against him. Closing his eyes, he put his arm over it and began to smile.

Peace was coming to him at last. And now he slept.

Rafe didn't hear the door swing open sometime later. He didn't know that someone was hovering over him until strong hands took him by the shoulders and shook him till his mouth flew open. "Wake up, bad boy! You done broke every rule of this house and put us all in danger. I got some bones to pick wit' you, and some spanking to do too."

"That's Mama's voice!" he shouted aloud as if he hadn't heard it in years. His bursting heart was so full of joy that he could think of nothing else but throwing his arms around her.

"Your mama's voice is right," she growled, shoving him off. "I'll give you your mama's voice and somethin' more too."

Hanna's mother, standing in the hall nearby with her daughter, said, "Rosalie, he's only a little boy."

"This little boy come upstairs without nobody givin' him the all clear. He leave the trapdoor wide open for any snoop to find it—which somebody almost did. Not only that, but he been told time and time again not to go in the crawl tunnel. But he go in, and he crawl all the way through into the graveyard, when Mr. Terwilliger gone to so much trouble to hide that end of it. Then, when this little boy finish, he put the lid back on wrong and leave his finger marks in the

69

dirt. If your husban' could make that out in the moonlight like he done, don't you think somebody else could?"

"Oh, Mama," Rafe cried, trying to wrap himself around her again.

"Don't you 'Oh, Mama' me. If Hanna's papa didn't go down there to check on everythin', he wouldn't have thought to come hot-footin' it back—and then he wouldn't have caught that man about to catch you! Oh, now you a-cryin'. That would do us a lot of good if you . . ."

In the dim glow of the candlelit hall, Rosalie saw her son's crushed face. There was such silent agony written on it that she turned to the others. "What's the matter wit' this boy that he can't take me givin' him a piece of my mind? I done it when he been bad before, and he never look like this."

"Rosalie," cried Hanna, "you're a-makin' him feel like he's the worst person there ever was!"

"Aw, he knows how tired I is."

"You pushed him away. He thinks you hate him!"

"No, I don't hate my son. Rafe, you think I hates you?"

"*Yes!*" Out of the corner of his eyes, Rafe looked at Hanna. She was strangely small and sounded different. But she was his friend again. Somehow he felt that she hadn't really been his friend for a long time.

"You doesn't really?" his mother asked again.

"Yes, I does."

"Oh, my sweet little lamb, you come back here to me. Ain't no way I could take back my love for you. Not ever. You just worry me, that's all." She clutched him, kissing his head. "And I gets so weary sometimes, sweetness, till I don't hardly know what I'm doin'."

70

"Mama, I'm gonna save you!"

"Oh, you are? Well, I think that's good. I'd like that just fine."

"I am, Mama. I am."

"Tell you what. We save each other, how is that? 'Cause you makes me feel so good sometimes, I forget all the evil things there ever was."

"Mama, I was wrong. I won't be wrong again."

"I know that, honey. You had the life scared out of you by that man on the other side of the door. Hanna's father tol' me all about it. He knew you were in here. He just waited for me to come back and deal wit' you. But now I think I shouldn't have done it like I did. So I was wrong too, and I won't be wrong again. You forgives me?"

"Mama, I want us to go away to Canada."

"We will, sweetness, we will. I'm going out just one more time, that's all."

"But that man say he goin' get a warrant to look for the hiding place."

"Let him look, baby. It going to be closed down by then. And you and me be long gone. I'm just going out one more day."

"But Mama, he say you gonna be taken back to Kentucky and they goin' prove you is Mother Freedom. They is a reward for you! He just need some judge to sign something!"

"Listen to what he's telling you, Rosalie," said Hanna's mother.

"Dora, hush now."

"But your work here is finished. Don't you see that?"

"*Tomorrow*, I say. I knows for sure somebody swam over on a barrel the other night. The minister took him part of

71

the way here in his ice wagon, but then he had to roll him off in the woods 'cause the patrols is out. If the man gets through on his own, he goin' to try to make it to the ice shed by the millpond. Tomorrow I'm going back to it, 'cause I cain't leave no poor soul out there without I takes him with us."

"Let *me* go for him!" cried Rafe.

"No, darling." She caressed his face. "You stay a little boy just a while longer. The time may come soon enough."

"Does I have to go back down to the hiding place now, Mama?"

"Yes, you do. But you know what?"

"What?"

"You makin' me feel so lonely that tonight I'm gonna spend the res' of it there wit' you. Come along now. Tomorrow night we leave for Canada. Tonight we is here. But anyplace Rafe Sims and his mama is together, that place is home."

SEVEN

It was the next afternoon. Rosalie was resting in her room for the dangerous night ahead. The children had been told to stay quietly in the hiding place while Mama and Papa Terwilliger were making plans to save the situation at the hotel. As part of those plans, the guests were being politely asked to leave. Mama had been going back and forth in the buggy for hours, driving them down to the wharf, where the steamboat *Heart of Dixie* would soon be pulling in. She had also loaded up a couple of shotguns. The captain, meanwhile, had gone with his lawyer to the courthouse to argue against the new law. And their daughter had been given a new role to play below: schoolteacher.

"Hanna," said Rafe after a while, "will you stop readin' me 'bout George Washington long 'nuff so I kin ask you a question that is just between you and me?"

She looked up from the writing desk. "What is it?"

"Does you ever get the feeling like you have been here before and you be doing everything all over again? Sort of so you kin get it right this time?" He paused to glance sideways at her. "Does *you* ever feel that?"

"Well, maybe. Sometimes, but—"

"You *has?*" he cried, jumping up excitedly. "That's the same as me ever since I went dreamin' in the crawl tunnel! You was dreamin' one time in there too. Mama said that you was. She was goin' take you to the Conjure Woman to figure the dreams out, only then she got sick. But your mama took you t' see her. So what I wants to know is—"

"I don't care to talk about the Conjure Woman," Hanna snapped. "And I don't care to think about any of that right now."

"Why not?"

"'Cause there was somethin' I didn't like in those dreams."

"Hanna, you kin tell me."

"It scares me."

"Well, I ain't scared of nothin', so you just take my hand and—"

"Maybe some other time."

"Some other time? Ain't you forgettin' that after tonight me and Mama is heading out for Canada?"

"Of course I'm not forgetting. I just . . . I just . . . hope everythin' goes all right, that's all."

He looked at her hard. "You don't think it will?"

"I ain't saying that," she cried, slamming *The Life of George Washington*, by Reverend Weems, down on the desk. "Don't go a-putting words in my mouth, Rafe Sims!"

There was a long silence. After a while they looked at each other more softly. "Hanna, you gonna miss me when I'm gone?" His eyes glinted damply.

"Li'l Rafe, are you going to up and cry now?"

"No."

"All right, then. See you don't." She stood up and started to walk around the little basement cell.

"Fine with me." There was another long silence. Rafe finally said, "Didn't you never want no brother?"

"A *brother*?" Hanna's face wrinkled up in disgust. "What

74

in the world would I do with one of *those*?"

"How should I know? But there he was."

"There *who* was?"

"Thought you said you didn't want to talk 'bout tunnel dreamin'?"

"Didn't say I wouldn't talk about *your* dreaming. I had a real cross-your-heart brother?"

Rafe shrugged. "Seemed he was."

"What was he like?"

"Pesky."

"Well, you see then? That's what I mean."

"Hanna, you don't want to tell me one little thing 'bout what you dream when you was in the crawl tunnel?"

"Nope."

"Why is that?"

"Well, it's on account of . . ." Hanna's lips began to tremble. She had to stop and start again. "On account of that's when I took the notion that pretty soon I was never gonna see my mama and papa again. Least not till they became . . ."

"Became what?"

In a small voice she said, "*Ghosts*."

He jumped back. "Ghosts!"

"Yes! Papa had only one arm because the other had been shot off. Mama had been so unhappy over losing me that she couldn't rest in her coffin for ever so long. Then I followed them back to my grave, which was a-waitin' empty for me till my body was found. I was crippled up and I had to slide down into my own tomb and . . ."

Rafe stared at her, wild-eyed with fright.

"Well, you asked me! Are you enjoyin' this, or kin we stop a-talkin' about it now?"

75

"I . . . uh . . . reckon we could—"

"Thank you so much!" Hanna started for the ladder. "I think I'll go see if Papa's back from arguing with the judge, and find out what's goin' on."

"I'll go with you!"

"No, you can't! You have to stay down here."

"*Alone?*"

"Oh, for goodness sake, they were *my* ghosts, Rafe, not yours!"

"How you know I ain't stuck with them now?"

She stared at him. "You're just a-doin' everything you kin to keep me down here with you, that's all. I do declare, Rafe, you're like a little baby. You can't be left alone for a second."

"No, I'm not a baby," he pouted. "You say that again and I'll hit you so hard . . ."

"Maybe you didn't know that I can hit back."

"Oh yeah! You want to wrassle with me now, see who's stronger?"

"No, I think that's stupid." She studied his unhappy face for a while. "But I'll stay, all right?"

Rafe shrugged. He watched her sit down across from him and put out her legs until their shoeless feet were up against each other. "I cain't believe you was using that *I do declare* stuff like you was some plantation lady," he said.

"I was just a-tryin' it out to see how it sounded."

"Sounded terrible."

"I know."

She pushed her bare feet against his and scrunched her longer toes down over Rafe's. It made them both feel better.

After a while, Rafe said, "You goin' let me take some of

Aunt Ida's cookies with me when I go?"

"I guess."

"Did she really make them all herself? Or did she have some slave to do it?"

"No, she made them. You know my mother won't take a thing that's been made by slaves."

"So how come your nice, sweet, good aunt keep any slaves at all?"

"She got them from my grandpa when he said he wouldn't leave them to Mama 'cause she'd only set them free. Since then Mama's been working very hard to show her that slavery is wrong. She's almost got her believing it now, and Aunt Ida's going to free all of them as soon as she dies."

"When she dies, how's she going to be able do anything?"

"Well, it'll say so in her will."

"Will? What's that?"

"It's a piece of paper with a big stamp on it."

"Suppose somebody tear up that paper with the stamp? Then what?"

"Rafe, nobody would do that!"

"Oh no? What about the piece of paper that was supposed to sell me back to my mama? The squire tore that up, didn't he, even after he was paid?"

Hanna thought about this a long time. "You know, that's true. I better write and tell Aunt Ida to free her slaves right away."

"Yes, I think you'd better. And that's one letter I will help you figure what to say."

"That's a good idea! Let's do it!"

❧   ❧   ❧

They were still trying to decide what to write when the trapdoor opened and the captain himself came down. "You children are entitled to know what's going on," he said. "So far I believe we're doing rather well. My attorney has gotten a paper that ought to stop anything from happening today. By tonight, after Mrs. Sims and Rafe are gone, we'll make sure this room can't be found. We may even close down the tunnel. That doesn't mean our work won't go on, of course. We'll simply find other ways to handle it."

Though he had spoken as if everything would be all right, Hanna could see the worry in his eyes. She knew how much he'd always loved this place. "Papa, are we goin' to lose the hotel?" she asked.

"I don't know whether it will be a hotel for a while, dearest." His big brown mustache lifted over a tender smile as he touched her hair. "But it will always be our home. Don't you fret about that."

Rafe's question cut deeply into that smile. "What about you all maybe goin' to jail?"

"Let's hope it doesn't get to that point," declared Dora Terwilliger, following her husband down the ladder. "But if it does, we'll take what comes and bear up like soldiers. Just as your mother would."

To Rafe, Mrs. Terwilliger—wispy-thin as she was— somehow looked more powerful than the captain. "Now I think I owe somebody a very good supper. Coming right up. I mean down." She turned from the ladder to look at them all. "That was supposed to be funny. It would be considerate if somebody chuckled at least."

"I'm laughin', Dora," boomed a voice just above them.

"Oh, Rosalie, you're awake?"

"'Course I'm awake. Hanna, you come upstairs and get dressed in your finery. Soon as the sun goes all the way down, we get our move on to the millpond. Quicker we there, quicker we get this over with."

"Mama, I'm goin' with you this time!"

"No, you ain't. Don't you be startin' that again, you hear?"

"Yes'm."

"That's my good boy."

To Rosalie's "good boy," every hour he was left alone in the hiding place was a misery of waiting and worrying and having nothing to do.

Hanna's talk about her tunnel dream of ghosts didn't help him either. He'd been sitting at the writing desk not more than an arm's reach from the flickering lantern. Now he pulled it nearer, telling himself that if some old spirit was going to be a-comin' through a wall, it would prob'ly be just about this time of the night, when everything was so still.

Crrrack! The sound came from above. The hatch flew open. Mrs. Terwilliger's face hung over it, and she was breathing hard. Was that a shotgun in her hand? Behind her stood the captain, with a hammer.

"Darlin', put out the lantern, but don't be afraid," Mrs. Terwilliger said. "We won't let them find you, I swear! A posse of men is galloping up the road, and Amos has to nail this hatch down, then put furniture over it. But we promise to let you out and get you to your mother as soon as they are gone."

"Where my mama?" Rafe shouted. "Where she at?"

"Still away with Hanna, thank God! Rosalie knows better than to come back into a trap. And we're going to make things so hot for these roughnecks before they get inside, she'll hear the noise a mile away."

Rafe now clearly saw the shotgun gripped in her hand. In a flash he had a vision of other guns—hunting rifles with long thin barrels going off in wooded darkness near a dried-out creek.

"They goin' to kill my mama!" He rushed to the steps. "I has to be with her. I come back to protect her! The ghost . . . she wants me to save my mama!"

Mrs. Terwilliger turned in dismay to her husband. "Oh, Amos, he's talking so wild!"

Now the face of the captain appeared. "Rafe, please listen. The one thing that would completely destroy your mother would be if we let something happen to you. We all love her, and we also care for *you* very much. Our Hanna is at risk too. So please, please cooperate and trust that we will do everything we can. Now you may hear noises up above. Do not under any circumstances make a sound yourself."

The hatch cover closed. Rafe heard the quick rapping of the hammer, then the sound of heavy furniture being moved and set down. He was sealed off from the house.

Where was his mother? What should he do? His mind was still in a puzzle when he heard Hanna's distant calling from the tunnel.

"Rafe, where are you?"

"Here!"

She must have been scurrying along quickly. The dark shape of her head soon appeared. "Why's the lantern out?"

"Your mama said to put it out. She don't want nothing coming from here. She say there are men fixing to come into the hotel. Where's my mama?"

80

Hanna stood up. "She sent me to come git you. You ready?"

"Girl, that ain't no kind of question. I was 'bout half ready to go by myself. Only how would I know where my mama was at? Let's go."

He had already dropped to his knees when he heard her gasp as if something had suddenly alarmed her. Looking back, he saw her grope for the ladder.

"What you doin'?"

"I have to see Mama and Papa!"

"You crazy? You cain't go up there!"

"I got to! I have to say good-bye."

She sounded desperate, but he couldn't understand why. "What you sobbin' for? You goin' see them when you gets back."

"I won't! I know I won't. I won't see them again. Not forever and ever!" She'd been pressing on the hatch, but it wouldn't budge. "It won't open!" She started hitting it. "Oh, why won't it open?"

"'Cause they put something over it to make it harder to find, that's why."

She was pounding on the hatch now. "Rafe, help me. I've got to see them. Mama!" she screamed. "Mama! Let me come up! Oh, Mama, please. I can't go off like this. Please open it!"

She's been tunnel dreamin' again, thought Rafe. That's what this is. That's what made me talk so wild to Mrs. Terwilliger too. But why am I cryin' here like some helpless li'l baby myself when I ought do somethin' to help my frien'?

He tugged at her foot. "Hanna, you listen here. I'll go myself. You just tell me where my mama is at."

Hanna hurried down the ladder. "Do you mean it? You'd go without me?" She had taken his hand in hers, and now she put it to her face, where the tears were. "When you come out through the cemetery," she sniffed, "you just turn to the right."

Here he was, being so ignorant again! But what could he do? *Right* is which?

She touched one shoulder, saying, "It's this arm. You go where this arm will be. Only that's if you climb out facing front. If you're facing backward . . . oh, you won't get it!"

This was too much. Here he was making it easy for her, but she was insulting him. "You take me for a fool! Shore I will. This way if I come out front. That way if I come out back. What else?"

"Then you don't let anybody see you and keep going till you come to the schoolteacher's cabin."

"How long it take me?"

"I don't know. Not long. First you cross the creek. Well, the creek will be dry now, so you won't see any water there. But you go down it and then you go up the other side."

She came closer, as if she was trying to make out from his face whether he was getting this. But before he could say *Girl don't waste my time!* she went on: "The cabin is right near there. And there's a big water bucket in front of it." She fell silent. "But if you get lost in the dark . . ."

"Shoot, I never gets lost in the dark. I'm goin'."

"Rafe, are you sure?"

He didn't answer her. He was already in the tunnel.

He couldn't know as he crawled along that Hanna was already starting to regret letting him go off on his own, or that in another moment she would set off after him, trying

82

desperately to catch up. How could he know that she'd just had another vision of her own . . . a vision of three men with long Kentucky rifles crouching in the graveyard, where they had silently followed her. A vision of Rafe not knowing he was leading them to Mother Freedom.

A vision of murder.

EIGHT

The narrow space grew even smaller. Some clods of earth seemed to have fallen near the end of the tunnel. Rafe crawled on his belly with his elbows tucked underneath, his fingers scratching the earth to pull him ahead while his toes pushed. Here was the deepest darkness of all, and it was only when his nose touched up against wood that Rafe knew the graveyard was just above him. The barrel hoop that served as hatch cover would have been easy to move by itself if it hadn't been hidden under earth and brush. The boy had to shove with the top of his skull as well as his hands before it gave way.

One day—perhaps very soon—this lid would be hidden deeper, at the bottom of a young girl's open tomb. But for now it only had to be lifted a few inches to the surface. Two darting eyes came up to ground level and looked about at the trees and bushes. There was nothing to see. No one could be crouching behind those tiny slabs that marked the places where the earliest white settlers of the wilderness were turning to dust.

Rafe knew this was no time to be in a tremble about ghosts. It was of the living that he had to be fearful. Yet there was nothing to hear, either, not the rustle of an owl, not even a summertime cricket. The complete silence should have warned him, for nature is hardly ever still. But he had to get a move on, and he sprang to the ground. Mother Freedom—*she* was really the hunted one!

Now which was his right arm again? This one. And which way had he just come out? Got it. Don't get lost now, he told himself, plunging into the woods. Go straight as you kin to that creek, straight like an arrow, even with the trees. No telling how soon someone goin' find out Mama ain't at the hotel. Maybe some of 'em ain't even waiting to share that reward money for taking her dead or alive!

A horrible thought came over him. Supposin' the schoolteacher's cabin was already surrounded! Mama had a pistol, but what if the men were on all sides of her? What could he do then to defend and protect her?

With his mind so a-buzz with racing thoughts, Rafe might not have been paying enough attention to the now-and-then sounds of dry twigs being broken underfoot. But then again, they pretty nearly matched his own steps. How could he suspect that behind him—almost as silent as shadows—were three white men in moccasins?

What kin I do, he was still asking himself, when these fists is so small and puny they cain't do nothin' 'gainst no big strong men?

Then he thought of David and Goliath.

That's it! Ain't nobody better'n me at hitting what I aim at!

It was his dead stop and a twist to hunt for rocks that did it. Out of the corner of his eye, he caught movement behind him about twenty feet back. It could have been a deer that had ducked behind that big tree, or even a bear. Maybe it was a bobcat or a panther, though they went mostly on the branches. It could even—this gave him a shiver—be some old ghost whose grave he'd stepped on who had followed him out of its resting place. That notion was scary, though he could handle it. But what if it was a *man?*

What if he was leading someone to his mama? Rafe's body was a-tingle now as his brain filled with a vision of the last time he had lived through all of this. The memory made him clutch the big rock in his hand all the harder.

It also made him move on, but not quite the same way. He was being followed, so he had to lead whoever it was in the wrong direction. Had to do it till he lost the . . . the *three* of them, he remembered. Yes, three white men who he somehow knew could move quieter than the wind in their Indian moccasins. Three trackin' men of the southland who had long huntin' rifles. He had to shake them off, and *then* get to her. If he couldn't shake them off, then he'd still take them the wrong way, even if he never did see his mama again.

It was this thought that made him wipe his eye as he went along, although he choked back the sob so it wouldn't make a sound. Still, the back of his shoulders gave a twitchy little jump. Perhaps *that* was what the men noticed.

"Fixing to kill somebody with yore rock?" whispered a voice from behind a tree next to him. There was no time for fear. Rafe's throwing arm whipped back as he whirled around to face the enemy.

But from behind him, like the spring of a cat onto fallen leaves, a powerful arm was suddenly across his chest, pinning him.

The cold, hard edge of a hunting knife pressed against his throat, and a voice just as fierce growled, "Hold still, boy, so I kin cut yore throat. You die right here, right now, iffen you don't show us where she be."

The bolt of terror that shot through Rafe was like an act of mercy. It overran his brain, blotting out all sound, all light, all awareness. He couldn't answer, no matter what they did to him. He couldn't know that his captors had no intention of killing him. No fugitive slave would be a worth a penny if returned to his master dead. Yet a split second after Rafe fainted, a rim of blood opened up across his neck. His slumping head had pushed too hard against the blade.

As the two other men darted by, the oldest said in a low voice, "Slap him awake afore he dies and see what you kin get out of him. Calvin, you swing aroun' that away. I'll keep a-goin' this."

Hanna had been faster than Rafe in squirreling through the long tunnel. She came out of it seeing the backs of the trackers as they followed the unwary boy out of the graveyard. She desperately wanted to call out for him to run. But then they might shoot him or capture and torture him. It was Rosalie who was in the most danger now, and Hanna knew a roundabout but quicker way to the schoolteacher's cabin. She streaked across the graveyard to the huge meadow on the other side. Only then did she turn toward the right, as Rafe had done. Plunging through the woods and over a log bridge to the far side of the creek, she turned right again and raced madly along the bank, gasping for breath.

It was the back wall of the cabin that she came to first. Rather than lose another second, she threw herself against it, panting through the chinks in the logs, "Rosalie, trackers are coming!"

Mother Freedom rushed outside, her pistol drawn as she dashed up to Hanna. "Where's my Rafe?"

"Rafe's comin', but they're a-followin' him. Only that

don't make no nevermind, Rosalie, because . . . because . . . let me just ketch my breath . . . because, well, I know this sound crazy, but you got to believe me. I done saved him afore—though I don't remember 'xactly how. I just know I'll do it again. So you've got to go."

From the bushes nearby, Papa's nervous horse pawed the ground. The fugitive they'd found together that evening was already in the driver's box, holding the reins. He could not speak, but he waved to Mother Freedom to come away now.

"I ain't leavin' without my son!" Rosalie said. "Hanna, you takes this man farther north to the next stop. You knows where it is. If anyone stop you, make out like he your servant taking you for a visit, same like you'd a-done with me. You both git now. I'm goin' to find my—"

All at once, a rifle flashed with a loud crack. The horse reared, and, screaming in terror, slammed the carriage back into a tree. The fugitive in the driver's box fell forward so hard, he landed on top of the animal as it bolted away. That may have saved the runaway slave from capture, but it didn't help Hanna and Rosalie. A man was dashing down the side of the creek from the direction of the log bridge. The rifle in his hands cracked as he came running.

"Run, child. Git away from here fast!"

"I cain't go without Rafe. It ain't supposed to happen like this!"

"It's a-happenin'. Go!"

Rosalie tried to give her a push, but Hanna grabbed her arm, pulled and tugged, and pleaded in words she barely understood. "Rosalie, if you don't run, they'll kill you here again. Come with me now to the skip-ahead time. Please!"

"Leggo. I got to fight!" Yanking free, she pushed Hanna

out of the way to fire at the oncoming man just as he dove for a rock.

"How can I make you see that we both have to run?" Hanna screamed at her. "This is for *Rafe*! This is what he came back for! It was to save his *mother*!"

"Stop it, I cain't fight with you and them at the same time! This is an order! Do what I say!"

Hanna ran as Rosalie stepped between her and the two lines of fire. She ran knowing that instead of ducking for cover, Rosalie was letting herself become an easier target for her sake. She ran till she heard a cry of pain and then a whoop of joy. "Got her, Uncle! I got her."

Hanna turned to see Rosalie stagger, drop her pistol, clutch her left side, and fall. "Murderers!" Hanna screamed at the gloating men as she ran back toward them, her weaving finger pointing from one to the other. "Do you think getting rich on reward money will make you any better than you are? Well, it won't! You are lower down now than you ever were! You are the worst trash there is!"

The younger man's rifle wheeled in her direction, but the other bellowed at him. "You a-looking to be hauled t' jail, Calvin? Killing a white is against the law in any state I know of."

"So we dump her body where they cain't never find her, that's all. Folks kin suspicion what they want to, long as they cain't prove nothin'. T'ain't every day we ketches us a hellfire 'bolitionist."

"That's true," agreed the older man. "But listen here. Drunk or sober, we won't never say a thang 'bout no tunnel and a-seein' her go into it. That a-way cain't nobody show we knew anythin' 'bout her."

"Now yer a-talkin'!"

They had been staring straight at Hanna all this time. The horror of their icy coldness seemed to have frozen her legs. But little by little, Hanna forced herself to back away.

"Turn, girl, that's all right," said the uncle, spitting out a stream of tobacco juice. "Go on an' run. Calvin, ye want the shot?"

"Oh, age before beauty, I always say. You take it."

"I don' know. She's so small, and that was about the sweetest face I ever did see."

"*Sweet?* She called us everythang you could thank of!"

"T'aint her fault what her folks done taught her."

"Whyn't you just fess up how yore a-takin' pity on all kinds of dumb critters in your old age?"

"Callin' me *old?* I'll give you old."

Crack! The whoosh through Hanna's hair made her wild with panic. She tripped, stumbled over the edge of the dry creek, and fell. Down she tumbled to the rocky bottom, skinning her legs and elbows, bashing her nose.

"You missed her a'purpose," the younger tracker said calmly, as if there was all the time in the world while Hanna scurried to her feet.

"Mebbe so. I still cain't brang myself to kill a white. Not without a war, leastways. But she's down there in the gully. So you do now what you want."

"I aim to, soon as I reload."

Hanna could hear him coming down into the dry creek behind her as she ran. She should have gone into the woods, where the moonlight wouldn't make her so easy to see! How long would it take him to pour powder from his horn, drop a bullet into the muzzle, ram it down, and put the cap on? How long before he took aim? She'd seen deer hunters do it in almost no time at all.

The creek took a bend just ahead. Why, she knew that place, didn't she? Could this be where . . . ? If it was, there would be a kind of mist rising up from the ground, a strange fog that would swirl up around her and inside of her too. If only she could get to it in time . . .

She was almost there. She could see where the mist was starting to form, where Hanna would become Anna. There would be a second father and mother in that place, and a little brother, too.

A shot rang out that split the air.

Rosalie had begun to stir when the sound came echoing back. It filled her head so she could not make out the words being shouted back and forth. Her eyes were still trying to focus when she saw one man go down into the gully, calling back to the other.

Her side ached terribly, but the leg beneath it was beginning to feel numb. Everything about her felt weak, yet it was now or never. She had fallen on her wound, and first she had to roll out of the pool of blood until she was lying flat. Then, pulling her legs under her and pushing up with her hands, she slowly got to her knees. Now to stand, that was the harder part. When her hands left the ground, her body swayed and she began to topple. A low-hanging branch of a weeping willow saved her from falling. As she pulled herself up, she thought of the gun.

Need that to save my boy!

She wouldn't ask herself if he was still alive. 'Course he was. A mother would know that, wouldn't she? Still clinging to the weeping willow, she lowered herself until the revolver could be fished up. Staggering away, she tore a wide leaf from a bush and shoved it up under her soaking blouse.

There was another reason for this, besides trying to slow the bleeding. She had to slow down the trackers, too. Once they came back, they'd be looking for a trail of blood . . . touching the ground in the dark . . . tasting their fingers to make sure. Rosalie had told many a runaway who might get shot to eat each leaf before it was ready to drip, putting another one into its place.

Weak as she felt now, that gully seemed too hard to cross. She might never be able to go up the other side, and loose, falling stones could make plenty of noise. Best head for the log bridge, even if it was the longest way to go.

It was trying to think straight like this that was clearing her head. Now if only some of the strength in her body would come back. The six-shooting gun was feeling so heavy that it was like to drop from her hand if she didn't watch out. She staggered over the footbridge, then across the meadow. Going this way, she came into the woods from the graveyard the way her son would have done it.

As silently as any tracker, she came up behind the man who had stayed with her motionless son. He didn't hear a thing until the pistol pressed against his temple. She bent to his ear, and her voice came breathing in on him like a moaning wind. "I see the blood on your knife. You the one done kilt my son?"

"No, no! He's all right. Jest a slice on the skin is all, and even that's a-clogging up. Look! See? He ain't a-spurtin' like he would if the main line had done been cut."

"Then why ain't he breathin'?"

"But he *is*! Put your hand over his mouth. Moves too. Look, I'll show you. Lemme jes' give him a shove with my foot."

"You do and you dead."

Carefully she laid her hands on his chest. The little heart was beating. Her fingers lightly touched his lips.

Somewhere down inside his dreams, Rafe sensed the presence of his mother. In his struggle to come back to her, his mouth twitched slightly. His eyelids fluttered, though they didn't open.

"Oh, my dearest baby, Mama is here. I is here!" To the man, she said, "Where's your hoss at?"

"Out yonder near to the road," said the man, growing calmer now that he could look Rosalie over and see her gripping her side. "Only it's a long walk there from here, and you ain't never going to carry him far as that with that hole in you." He spat out a chaw of tobacco juice. "You give yourself up now, and I'll get him patched up real good."

"You'd best don't be stalling me no more. First sight I ketch of them other two, I shoots you dead. Pick him up. Both arms. Gentle now! Don't you let his head drop back."

She knew as they trudged along that he was counting on wearing her out. Meanwhile, she caught him using Rafe's outstretched feet to break twigs and leave a trail for the others to follow. When she told him to cut that out, he almost laughed at her. He knew how much she still needed him, and he was getting more sure of himself all the time.

She suspected that he was trying to stretch the distance out. Of course Rosalie knew better than he did where the old country road was. But it would be easy to shift just a little to this side or that and come out far from the horses.

"I know what you doin'," she finally warned him. "I'm goin' to count to twenty ten times. If we ain't to the horses by then, you finished for good."

"That ain't fair!"

"Don't you be tellin' me what's fair, slaver. Move it!"

"What for? One way or t'other I'm a dead man, ain't I?"

"Maybe yes, maybe no. But this way, for sure—and right now. Move!"

"All right, all right," he grumbled, setting out again.

"One, two . . . I say fast! Three, four . . ."

The two trackers walked back along the gully, shaking their heads. "If that don't beat all," said the younger one. "Just as I pull the trigger she ain't there no more. How'd she do it?"

"I don't know, Calvin. Don't much care, neither. Ye gave her the scare of her life, and that should be enough for ye. Let's pick up the woman's body and git on with business."

But their business suddenly took a hard blow when they came back to the place where Mother Freedom had fallen.

"This cain't be. I kilt her for shore," muttered the younger man.

"Is that right?"

"Maybe she just crawled off a little ways to die."

"If that's the case, why don't I see no sign of blood a-goin' away from here? Oh, she's a smart'un, I'll tell ye. But it won't help her none."

"Where do you think she went?"

"Well, if that was *my* little boy back with your brother, I know where I'd go. Come on."

❧   ❧   ❧

Rosalie was in the middle of her ten times twenties when the man carrying Rafe said edgily, "How many is that now?"

"Nobody ever learned you to count?"

"Mebbe not," he huffed. "But that don't make you better'n me."

"Your skin don't do it for you, neither. Keep goin'." She tried to sound strong, but the growing weariness was seeping into her voice.

He knows it, too, thought Rosalie, watching his back begin to tense. He was going to make his move, and soon. "Time's 'most up," she said, wanting to bring on the attack while she was still alert enough to deal with it.

But he was being sly. "We're real close to the horses now," he said. "If I whistle for mine, she'll stomp. Then the others will too, and you kin stop your dang countin'."

"Yeah, I knows what else you be whistlin' for. So don't."

The moment was coming, and still they waited each other out. All along, Rosalie's wound had been stiffening her left leg. By this time she was almost dragging it, and now her foot caught on a root. As if he had eyes in the back of his head, the tracker leaned to the side, and swung Rosalie's son around at her like a club.

The child's legs struck her in the face. She went down— but it was more to avoid hurting him than herself. Now he flung Rafe away and lunged at her. She fired, but it was too late. The bullet went over his shoulder. Powerful hands took her by the throat.

"Dead or alive, we git the same money fer you!"

His thumbs pressed hard into her windpipe. She brought the gun crashing down on his head, knocking him unconscious.

Gulping in air, Rosalie dragged herself to the bushes, where Rafe was lying on his back. She put her ear to his chest. His heart was still beating.

"That my *chile*. That's a *fighter*!"

This time there was no low-hanging branch Rosalie could use to help pull herself up. But the sounds she heard now sent a feeling of hope rising inside of her . . . a feeling that lifted her to her feet. There were indeed stomping horses nearby.

Rosalie was no hand at riding. She had driven many a buggy and buckboard, but only once had she been in a saddle. So which was the gentlest horse? It was hard to tell, since they were all big-eyed and soft-looking.

"I'll take the lowest to the groun', then," she mumbled aloud.

She realized that she couldn't leave the other two horses for the slavers to jump on and chase her. The pistol wove in her hand. "Precious Jesus," she prayed, "please understan' why I has to do this. There is no way I kin take a chance on drivin' them off. They'd prob'ly come right back on a whistle."

She was about to put the gun between the first horse's eyes when it lifted its nose to nuzzle her shoulder and gave the hand holding the gun a little love nip. Suddenly she brightened. "I'll pull the bridles off their necks to take with me, that's what I'll do! Not even trackers kin ride without those."

Throwing the bridles over the saddle horn of her own mount, Rosalie walked the horse over to Rafe. Yes, she had gotten that far. But to pick him up now and lift him into the saddle, how was she going to do that? And how was she going to keep him from falling off the other side while she tried to get on herself? It didn't seem possible when she was already so weak that she had to hold onto the horse to keep from falling.

But now came the sound of dry wood cracking under running feet and of bushes being knocked out of the way. It had to be the other trackers. They'd found that Rafe and their companion were gone. They'd picked up the trail and heard the shot. "Where are ye, Bo?" they cried. "Did you git her? Speak to us!"

At that moment, Rosalie threw herself at the child. Pain tore at her side as she tried to lift him, making her stagger back and almost scream. *This chile's mother kin take it!* she told herself, and heaved him up across the saddle.

The men were so close now, she could hear panting in the thick brush. "If she hurt my brother, I'll kill her fer shore!"

Pulling her gun out, Rosalie fired once into the bushes. Suddenly there was not a sound. But had she really slowed them? Putting her foot into the stirrup, she grabbed the saddle horn. Up she went, swinging her leg across while she snatched at the reins.

But then, oh the pain! Her side was on fire and the leaping flames scorched her brain! Even with the men charging madly for the road, her eyes slammed shut. Though blind for that moment, she kicked at the horse's side. It snorted, but that was all. She slapped its flank with the reins, but nothing happened.

"*Move!*" she roared, in a voice that had once driven a bear to give up its own cave. And the horse leaped ahead.

Its feet were pounding under her and her child when the

trackers burst onto the road, already too late to aim and fire. One man hurried to the horses, while the other one went to his fallen brother. "He's a-stirrin', Uncle Daniel, and so far I don't see no blood."

"Never mind that! Cut off his hair to the root! Then cut yours, too, and start braiding."

"*What?*"

"She done took the bridles! We got to make new ones out of our own hair. Get a move on. I aim to ketch that woman afore someone else finds her lying dead on the road and claims the reward fer himself!"

NINE

The horse Rosalie had taken was unhappy with strangers on her back, especially since one of them dangled over the bottom of her neck. And there was too much pulling on the corners of her mouth. Every time she twisted her head to shake free, she saw Rafe's flopping arms out of the corner of her eye. This strange sight made her fearful. She lowered her head and tried to run away.

The mare's sudden burst of speed made Rosalie bounce in the saddle and tighten her grip on the reins. That caused the metal bit in the mare's mouth to cut into her all the harder. In excitement and frustration, the mare threw her head back and whinnied. When answering whinnies came from behind her, the horse *knew* that her friends were coming after her. Now if only she could buck these strangers off!

Rosalie had been trying to sit Rafe up, but now it was all she could do to grab the saddle horn and hold on for both of them. The whinnies from behind were the worst news of all. The trackers were on their horses, still out of sight but coming on like demons!

She no longer believed she could get away from them. But the town was not far ahead now. After this next farm were a few houses, including the big house with the doctor's sign in front.

"Got to give him my boy without they see it! Then I rides on and fights them somewhere else."

There was the house, with a tiny lamp still on over the porch, in case someone had to come to him in an emergency. It was a miracle that she could still find the strength to call out, "Dr. Bertram, this is Rosalie Sims from the hotel. This is life or death."

An upstairs curtain parted. A rather sleepy but kindly voice said, "Who's hurting, Rosalie?"

"My son! He's here in my arms. They done cut his throat."

"Now listen to me," the doctor whispered, poking his head out and looking both ways. "Go back to the hotel. I'll get dressed and drive out there as if I am going to see Mrs. Terwilliger's little girl."

"Doctor, my son will be dead by then!"

"I'm truly sorry, believe me. But I would lose half my practice if the news got out that I treated a colored person in my office. There's one of your own ministers who practices a bit of medicine. Why don't you go to him?"

"That's twenty miles away. We never get there! I'm shot too."

"What were you involved in?"

"They after me 'cause I'm Mother Freedom! But this boy, he never did nothin' to anybody. And he got a whole life to live, if only—"

"I'm sorry. I cannot help you."

"But you is a doctor! You a healer! You wouldn't let a dog die like this!"

"Go away!" The window slammed shut.

Rosalie stood there with her child in her arms. Tears of rage came over her. She cried up to heaven, "Lord, is you goin' to let it end like this?"

"No, it mustn't!" cried a voice inside the house.

"Martha, you come back here. This is none of your business."

The door was flung open, and a woman in a shawl rushed out on the porch. "My husband doesn't mean what he's saying. Give him to me."

"Oh, ma'am, bless you! Yes, take my beautiful chile. I mus' leave quickly and lead them away from here."

But already there were hoofbeats coming down the road. Rosalie turned her head while they were both holding Rafe. The trackers, with their rifles lifted, were flying down the road, taking aim.

The doctor screamed, "Martha, look out!" His wife, suddenly frightened, fell back against the door, leaving Rafe still in his mother's arms.

Rosalie knew there was no escape. Still, she had to fight. For the last time, she kissed her little boy, then set him down on the porch and tugged at her gun. It hadn't left her belt before a rifle cracked. Rosalie's arms flew out to the side. She toppled backward, landed heavily, and was still.

As the horsemen rode up, the man who'd been sitting double leaped off. He stared at Rosalie's body and aimed a kick at it, then went to stroke his own horse.

His uncle paused in the saddle to bite off a plug of tobacco. Replacing it in his pocket, he touched his coonskin cap politely and said, "No need to be afeared of us, ma'am. What's this boy on your porch fer?"

"My husband is a doctor," she said, staring at him without blinking.

"Well, good. Would you please get him on down here?"

"Samuel?" she called.

"Sir, I am retired for the night," came a voice from behind a curtain. "You are officers of the law, I take it?"

"Yes, sir, we been deputized. This here was a wanted woman and she was shot legal while resistin' arrest, as you kin see. We're a-goin' to bring her body to the courthouse so she can be 'dentified in the morning afore we take her back to Kentucky. Now come on down like a good feller and patch this here boy up. He's a fugitive and I got charge of him till I get him back to his rightful owner, Squire Partridge, on the other side. I'll lay out the fee and pay ye extra if ye make him whole agin. There warn't no intention of hurtin' him. That were an accident from the situation. And as for what just happened, we're mighty sorry your missus had to see it. But we had no choice 'cept to defend ourself when she went to fire on us."

"Sir, I am most heartily sorry that I cannot be of assistance in this matter. But, you see, I have patients who agree with slavery and others who do not. It would seem as if I was choosing sides if I did anything to help you take him across the river to—"

"Samuel," cried his wife. "I cannot believe that you would rather let him die!"

"Very well. Bring him inside and put him on the operating table. I'll be right down."

"Boys," said their uncle, climbing down and heading for the house, "tie Mother Freedom on the mare so she won't fall off, and don't let anybody come an' steal her."

He came out again a few minutes later, shaking his head.

"What's the matter, Uncle Daniel? Is he dead?" Bo asked.

"Close to it. Tomorrow we'll come an' check on him. Shore would hate to lose the money. Squire Partridge may be cheap, but any boy with some years ahead of him is goin' to be worth three, four hundred at least."

"I'm sorry I warn't more keerful with him," said Bo. "But the happy side is we goin' to get rich on this one." He slapped Rosalie's back.

"No, I wouldn't say rich. But she'll pay off the farm, all right, and then some. Mount up."

The doctor's wife watched them ride away, then went back to her husband. "You have blood on you," he said.

"It will wash out, Samuel. The blood on their hands won't. While you finish sewing him, I'll get the buggy ready to take him to the Conjure Woman."

"What the devil are you saying?"

"Samuel, look at him. He won't last the morning here."

"Oh, I see. I am a scientist, but a person who cannot read or write—a witch doctor—will save him?"

"There are witch doctors who are false, my husband, but *she* works powerful medicine. She knows the spirits, magic, barks and plants, remedies of the forest—things that I saw as a child among my own people."

"That's just the point! There have been rumors enough about your being part Indian."

"If these rumors distress you, I will leave this house and never come back," Martha said.

"No, no! How can you threaten me with that when I love you so? Don't you know that I have only been trying to protect you from nasty, vicious tongues?"

"Samuel, I saw my own village burned down to the ground by men who claimed to have the white man's law behind them!"

"Exactly! Martha, these men are dangerous ruffians.

Sometime tomorrow they'll be back, and they'll insist on seeing the boy!"

"Then together, Samuel, we will show them where we buried his body."

"What if they demand we dig him up?"

"Then, my husband, I will call down my people's curse on all those who disturb the dead. And you will hand them a shovel."

The hundred-year-old Conjure Woman showed no surprise when Rafe was brought to her shack in the woods just outside the other end of town. She seemed to have been getting ready for him. A mat of clean straw had just been laid down over soft pine needles on the flat ground. The great pot in which she brewed her leaves and other medicines already sat steaming over a wood fire nearby. At a sign from the old black woman's crooked fingers, the doctor's wife carried Rafe close to the pot. Though he barely breathed, the sharp-smelling fumes entered his nose and went deep into the boy's lungs. When he jerked slightly, the Conjure Woman motioned to let him down on his back.

With a sharp stick she brought out a dripping leaf, let it cool a few moments, and brought it to his lips. Then she laid it over the deep cut on his neck and went for another.

"Is it too late?" the doctor's wife asked in a trembling voice. "Can you help him?"

"I cain't say yet, but I tells you this. The spirits—the Great One and the little ones—dey hears the languages of all the races. You kin chant in yours if you wants. Dance too. Dat way, you ease your own heart. Den we both be in the right place to be the healers of this chile. You ready?"

"Almost. But I—I can't stop seeing his mother being shot down in front of my home! Is there anything you can do for her?"

The old woman looked at her sternly. "Don't you never ask me to bring back the dead. That is one magic I won't never do. The dead don't need comin' back!"

"I'm sorry if I—"

"No, you ain't made me mad. You jest wants things to be the way they cain't. What I *am* goin' do, though, is put somethin' Rosalie Sims has touched in the fire and see what I kin 'bout her. If there is the littlest spark of life in Mother Freedom yet, we'll see what we can do to make a fire out of it. Only first we got to make the blood in this boy grow. Dance now, Running Deer. It was the spirits which love you that brought him to your door."

TEN

It was a few hours before daylight when the trackers brought Rosalie's body into the center of town. They stopped in front of its only tavern while one of them went inside to look for the agent from the slaveowners association that had offered the dead-or-alive reward for her.

The bar had stayed open all night because of the excitement, and some drinkers came out to gape at the body. But the search back at the Terwilliger Hotel must have still been going on, since neither the agent, nor the sheriff's posse, nor the U.S. marshal, had come back from it.

About half the men standing around were against slavery. Not even those who were for it cared to see a woman's corpse thrown over a horse like a hunted-down animal. Though none of these men were armed like the trackers, there were a lot of angry looks. The trackers were unafraid, but they left word for the agent to come to the courthouse and rode slowly away, spitting. Nobody was paying them to get into fights with Yankees. Someday maybe, if there was a war . . .

When they came to the courthouse, they carried Rosalie to the big front door, but it was still locked for the night. So they set her down on the top of the stairs, then squatted on the steps below and began to smoke.

"Sure wish we'd bought us some sour mash back there," said Calvin.

His grinning brother went to a saddle bag and came back with a small jug. "Surprise! Surprise!" he said. "I was savin' this one all along for a little celebration."

"Pass it on over here!"

"It's all right to wet our whistles, boys, but no more'n that till business is took care of. Meantimes, we got to look sharp. Case ye didn't notice back there, this ain't 'xactly home."

"Don't worry, Uncle Daniel." Calvin stopped to pull the cork out with his teeth. "Ain't nobody goin' to git anywheres near this prize."

The three men settled down to wait. Just before dawn they heard a strange clinking. A covered wagon pulled up in front of the courthouse, drawn by a very slow old horse. A gray-haired black man sat at the reins.

"Excuse me, gentlemen. May I ask if you would care to buy any ice?"

The leader of the trackers cocked an eye at him. "Ice? What would we do with it?"

"Perhaps put it next to that body, so it doesn't begin to smell after the sun come up."

"Git on, now."

"Yes, sir, but I am also a minister. If you don't mind, I would like to read a passage from the Bible over the departed."

"You kin *read*, nigger?"

"Very important to, sir. Otherwise some slave catchers would drag me across the river, even though I am a free black man with papers to prove it. Nobody over there wants a slave who can educate other slaves, so I make sure I keep the Bible close by. Now, sir, pray allow me to say some words from the good book over this woman. Otherwise her soul might refuse to leave her body and go to its rest. Then like Lazarus, who lay in his grave for four long days, she might rise from the dead."

"The dead don't rise. You get away from us, y' hear?"

"Indeed I shall. But if you please, sir, let it be after I make my delivery of a block of ice here."

"In the courthouse?"

"Yes, for the ice chest in the kitchen. That's through the side door in the back, and I have this key to it. The judge wants fresh ice once a week. It certainly won't do to make him angry."

"Bo, go with him. He's a sly one. Keep an eye on him, then kick his backside out of here."

"All right, Uncle Daniel, but I ain't helpin' him carry none."

"Just this one verse from the Corinthians, Chapter 15," said the ice man before he turned away. "'How say some among you that there is no resurrection of the dead? For if there be no resurrection of the dead then Christ is not risen!'"

"Git out of here, with your risin' of the dead, or we goin' to try that out on you and see how it works!"

"Whatever you say, sir," declared the minister, going over to his horse and leading it around to the back.

Just then, the doctor's wife drove up in her husband's buggy, looking as if she carried very bad news. "My husband sent me to tell you that he tried very hard, but . . ."

Uncle Daniel stood up quickly. "The boy's dead, and he's afeared to be a man and come out to tell me hisself." The tracker moved closer and stared at her. "You're an Indian, ain't ye?"

"That's right, and I am proud of it."

"Then why have ye been a-hidin' it?"

She tossed back her head. "Not any longer."

"What's your real name?"

"Running Deer."

"Well, Running Deer, I don't have any problem with Indians, now that we beat 'em fair and square. I like the way you stand up fer yourself."

"Uncle Daniel! Uncle Daniel!"

"*What?*"

"Thet body jest moved!"

"Why, Calvin, you let that crazy preacher git to ye. How kin ye be that dumb?"

"I'm a-tellin' you it's true. Look! It moved agin! The eyes are openin'. It's a-standin' up!"

"So shoot it agin," said his uncle without bothering to turn around.

From around the side of the courthouse came the recited words of an old man bent under a heavy block of ice. "'I am the resurrection, sayeth the Lord.'"

Thump, thump, thump. Rosalie walked down the wooden steps and right past the trackers. She did not look at them or anything else. Her eyes were sightless and blank, her legs stiff. Her feet hardly seemed to touch the ground, and her arms stuck partway out from her body. She moved as if she were being held up on both sides or dangled from above.

Perhaps she was.

Rosalie had been in a different kind of motion just moments before, only her body had not been a part of it. Her spirit found itself going down a long, wide tunnel. She was just coming to the end of it, where a powerful light was blazing, when a shadowy form moved in front of the opening.

"You still got the choice," the Conjure Woman said. "You don't have to leave yet."

"Please let me by, so I kin rest at last," Rosalie replied. "I has been through so much. Don't tell me now I still have some life to go."

"Oh, nobody is a-sayin' that Rosalie Sims cain't go through the pearly gates right now and be welcome. So could Mother Freedom, but ain't she still got her work to do?"

"Why does you have to ask me that? I cain't take care of everyone who runs off to be free! They is others back there to get them out. There is Harriet Tubman. There's Dora Terwilliger. There is—"

"There is Rafe Sims too. That boy done come back from being safe in another time to be with you, to help you. Only he too small yet to carry on by hisself in all that is a-comin'."

"Old woman, what you talkin' 'bout? Them trackers done kilt my son! I had to leave him to bleed to death when no doctor would help him! Now I got two bullets in me already. I don't need no more excuse to go to join my son!"

"Not down here, you won't, Rosalie. Your boy be back at my shanty. He don't know it yit, 'les it's in his dreams, but he comin' along real fine on this side of life."

"Is that the honest-to-God truth of it? You ain't jest sayin' this to get me to go back?"

"When ever did I tell you some lie, Rosalie? Your Rafe got the spark of life in him yit. And I don' care how weary you is, you does too! I wouldn't be here otherwise. So you just

110

decide right now, or else I'm goin' to git out of the way."

"If . . . if I goes back then how'm I goin' to deal with them trackers?"

"One thing at a time. Turn around now."

"I'm tryin', but I ain't floatin' no more."

"No, this is harder, 'cause you still at the doorway to death, back there. The onliest way your body is going to rise up and walk away is to lean your soul on the spirits. They be stayin' with you fo' a while. Just lean on them and let your body rise. There you go! You doin' it."

"But I don't feel them."

"Don't have to. Just be willin' is all. There! You already on your feet, even if you cain't tell that yet. Now they goin' to git you down the courthouse steps and into that ice wagon. That minister, he don't like havin' nothin' to do with witch doctors. But this time, he making a 'ception. Now that's it, you almost to the wagon."

"Well, what about the trackers? Ain't they putting any new bullets into me?"

"Not yet. You best keep a move on. One more hole in you and there ain't nobody goin' to be able to help you no more. Right now the white boys just starin' like the fear of God is on 'em. But that Uncle Daniel, he don't fear nothin' fer long. He already startin' to point his gun at you, so I'm a-countin' on Runnin' Deer. Oh, there she go now, foamin' at the mouth like she comin' down into a fit. Oh my, she fall right outten her buggy onto the uncle. Well, good fo' her. But she better watch out, though, for all that her eyes is a-rollin' and her teeth a-clackin'. He sweet on her."

"Who's Runnin' Deer?"

"Indian gal that the doctor married. Now don't sag, Rosalie! Push you legs hard."

"Is they shootin' at me yit?"

"Not yit. You're in the ice wagon now."

"It's cold!"

"The grave is colder, Rosalie, so don't you take on so. The freezin' will keep what's left of your blood from a bubblin' out till the operation."

"Who's goin' to do that?"

"Well, I ain't. Never did know how, and now I don't have the steady hands for it. The preacher might give it a try after he calms down. Or Runnin' Deer, who be a nurse for her husband time to time. Now I'll say good-bye, Rosalie. Got to git back inside of my own body."

"Wait! Don' go yet!"

"Oh, the spirits will stay with you awhile longer, till you wakes up . . . or till you don't. I cain't say fo' sure you goin' to make it. But whichever it goes, we all did our best, didn't we? That's all anybody kin ask."

"Yes,'m," answered Rosalie, letting go of her worries all at once, as a child might have done, and sounding to herself like a very little girl. As a grown woman, she had done all she could. Now, while the wagon moved slowly along, she could sink down to a place where it seemed that her own sweet mama's arms were always still open to her. It was down in here where the bad old world was far away that Rosalie could nestle and trust and feel so safe, so very safe. . . .

The three trackers had been too stunned at first to do any-thing to halt Rosalie's eerie march to the wagon. Then, just as they were clearing their heads long enough for the uncle to raise his gun, Running Deer had jerked up from her seat, madly shrieking. Her eyes rolled up into her head, her body twitched, and foam poured out of her mouth. Suddenly, before Uncle Daniel could fire at the departing wagon, she fell like a tree on top of him, clutching him with arms that felt like steel.

While the wagon was rolling out of sight, Bo sprang at Running Deer with his knife. "Leave her alone," cried the muffled voice of his uncle, struggling to break free of her crushing embrace.

"Uncle Daniel, that were a trick to let them git away."

"Mebbe so," grunted the uncle from underneath. "But I seen fits afore, and she couldn't git this strong without there being something real to it." With a final push he heaved himself out from under her. "Anyways, I like this woman, most especially if she done it a-purpose. She has all kinds of spunk." He got to his feet. "Now, boys, let's git mounted."

Young Bo scratched his head. "I'll tell you the truth, Uncle Daniel. I don't rightly know how I feel about going after the risen dead."

"Well, this is how I feel about it. She warn't dead after you shot her the first time, and I see now she warn't dead after I done it the second. But even supposin' she was dead, that woman is our money in the bank, and I don't care 'bout anything else. Iffen we have to tie down a corpse and sit on it to keep it from gettin' up, then that's what we're a-goin' to do. Now, that wagon is the slowest thang that ever moved. We could ketch it just a-runnin' on our own feet. So mount up, boys. Let's git."

Running Deer scrambled to her feet the moment the trackers were gone. Climbing into the buggy, she shook the reins and was off at a gallop in the direction of her house.

The doctor had been outside, nervously pacing back and forth as he waited for her. "What happened?" he demanded in terror as she leaped from the box and raced past him to the porch. "Have you seen them? Are they coming behind you? Are they going to make me dig up the grave?"

"I don't know," she cried, racing through the door. "I doubt it. I can't stop to think about it." Darting into his office for his medical bag, she immediately began stuffing it with a scalpel, forceps, clamps, soap, bandages. . . .

"What are you doing?" the doctor shouted at her.

"Isn't it obvious? I'm going to operate on Rosalie Sims."

"But those ruffians took her with them!"

"Well, they don't have her now!"

He threw his hands up. "This is beyond my understanding!"

"Perhaps it's beyond what you want to understand. Samuel, I'm going," Running Deer said, closing the bag and turning to walk past him. "There are many good hiding places in this house. I'm sure you can find one to keep you safe for a few hours."

He followed her to the door. "Where is she now?"

"I'm sorry," she said, hurrying across the porch, "but it's better I don't tell you so they can't get it out of you."

"Martha!" Running down the steps, he grabbed her arm.

She yanked free of him. "That was never my true name."

"You haven't the slightest respect for me, have you?"

"Not tonight," she said bitterly. "Not when you turn a bleeding child away from our door because someone might see the color of his skin."

"You are not going!" he cried, jumping between her and the carriage.

114

"Yes, I am."

"Let me finish what I meant to say! Martha . . . Running Deer . . . you are not going without *me*."

She stared at him. "*You* will do it?"

"Yes, of course," he whispered, lowering his head and turning away because there were tears in his eyes. "I have been feeling nothing but shame."

Running Deer softened at once. "Then come with me, my husband." She gave him her hand, and they ran together to the buggy.

The slave trackers on their thundering horses soon caught up to the ice wagon. But it had stopped. There was no one inside it, and the old nag in the harness was peacefully nibbling grass at the edge of somebody's front lawn. The street was empty, but footprints on the pathway led to the door of the house. When they pounded on it, a black man appeared, wearing the robes of a Catholic priest.

His huge size blocked the whole doorway, and he glared at them from under bushy white eyebrows. He already knew who they were and what they wanted. He barked into their faces in a thick French accent. This house in which he lived was church property, and therefore it was holy ground. And where the ground was truly holy, anyone who was helpless and wounded and in flight from injustice deserved to find sanctuary. Deputies or not, the only way they would come in to search this house was over his dead body.

The trackers let him go on like this only long enough to test the windows and an outside cellar door, which was locked. Bo was ready to jam his rifle butt into the priest's belly, until his uncle stopped him and pointed to a balcony above. Bo gave his brother a boost. Then Calvin pulled him up, and they both plunged into the house.

Meanwhile the uncle remained eye to eye with the priest. "You're a-pullin' somethin', ain't ye? They ain't a-goin' to find her in there, are they? Come on, let me hear how a man of God can lie."

The priest said nothing.

"I thought so. Boys!" he shouted past him. "I'm a-goin' round to the other side."

Dashing behind the house, he saw the back of the church. Between the two buildings was a garden and a stable. Uncle Daniel rushed to the stable. It was empty. Quickly examining the ground, he found fresh wagon tracks that led to the road in front of the church. He shouted for his nephews to come out of the house, get the horses, and catch up with him. Meanwhile he ran ahead, checking the wheel marks in the dirt road.

But roosters had been crowing for the last twenty minutes, and the town was wide awake and already going about its business. A grocer and the barber had hitched up and were driving to their shops. A lawyer in long tailcoats went by on horseback, heading for his office at the county seat. A group of men walked down the road toward the mill at the river's edge. The tracks were getting mixed together.

When the other trackers caught up with him, the uncle mounted his horse, and they all searched together. These men were too good at what they did not to pick up the trail, but it took a while to do it. Meanwhile, a heavy rain began to fall. Pretty soon it would wash everything away.

"Sure been havin' us some mighty strange luck," murmured one brother to another. "First, that girl I was

116

a-aimin' at done vanish on me. Then all this rising of the dead and folks havin' fits. You reckon they's a hex been put somewhere's on us?"

Their uncle turned on them with fire in his eyes. "I don't believe that, and I wouldn't give a hoot and a holler even if there was! Now you two git back to that ice wagon. Pull that horse away from the grass and watch where he goes. He's a-goin' to head fer home, boys, where his hay is and it's dry. You jest follow behind."

"But it don't stand to reason he took her there," Bo protested.

"Do like I say. Maybe he's got a family back there. Then you tie 'em up and set there and wait. But iffen there's nobody, you wait anyway. Iffen you see he ain't coming back at all, set fire to it. If he's really a minister, some of his flock are gonna come a-runnin' to put it out. Make 'em understand that unless you get some answers real quick, you'll drive 'em all across the river to be sold off! Now somebody's goin' to be real scared, only he won't want to talk in front of the others. So you take 'em each aside one by one and find out where's the best places to go a-looking."

"What are you a-goin' to do, Uncle Daniel?"

"What do you think? I'm a-headin' back to the doctor's house. His wife won't be there, I'll lay a bet on that. But iffen her husband ain't neither, then I'll know who's a-cuttin' the bullets out of our prisoner." The uncle wheeled his horse around and galloped off.

ELEVEN

Weeks had gone by since Anna and the Post family had gone back home without Rafe. Nothing was the same for her. The fun had gone out of life. She took no interest in her friends or her school activities, just moped around the house and cried. The tears came most often when she forgot that Rafe was no longer with them. She'd wake up and call out to him, or go down the steps to the kitchen expecting to find him sitting at the table gobbling breakfast—only he wouldn't be there.

Slouched over her homework one rainy evening, Anna doodled with her pen, hardly noticing what she was drawing. Slowly the head of a boy began to appear on the page. It was not a very good sketch of Rafe, yet it was real enough to make her gasp. A terrible sadness shone in his eyes. They were so very wide and so scared and unhappy. He might have watched his mother dying with just this kind of look, she thought. And what was that line across his neck? Was it a scar? Had someone taken a knife to him and . . .

Anna choked up. She pushed the drawing aside and tried to go back to her studies. But somehow she had the feeling that those suffering eyes were *watching her*, and waiting. Waiting for what? What was it the boy in that drawing wanted from her? Did he need her help?

Anna shoved the sketch deep into a drawer. She couldn't bear to have him calling out to her this way. Not when there was nothing she could ever do again for Rafe.

For days now Anna had been thinking about that drawing and feeling like a coward. How could she possibly care about Rafe and not want to share what he had been going through? As soon as she got home from school one afternoon, she marched to her room and yanked the drawing from the drawer.

Was there something about the light in this room that was making her eyes play tricks on her? Anna pulled the reading lamp close, turned it on, and held the drawing up to the light.

"Oh, my God!" she whispered, staring at the tight little smile on Rafe's lips. "It's changed!"

Dropping like a stone into her chair, she bent over the picture and ran her fingertips slowly over it.

Rafe's smile was not exactly a happy one, but it was brave. She still saw darkness in his eyes, and that smoky look she had often seen when he was close to being furious. But now there was a different kind of flash in them. A prouder look. She could almost hear him saying to her, *Girl, don't worry about me. I'll be all right.*

Anna wanted to believe that this was real, not some trick that her mind was playing on her. What would it hurt if she decided she *would* believe it? She felt like drawing a picture . . . of Rosalie.

Yet somehow this was much harder to do. Those nightmares she'd been having of seeing Rosalie get shot were scaring her. Just don't let them! she told herself. Yet drawing after drawing became nothing more than scribbles.

Anna was about to give up when the telephone rang. The caller left a long message for her mother. While Anna talked, her hand kept moving. When she hung up, *there* was Rosalie.

Anna couldn't look directly at the drawing at first. In fact, her hand was still filling everything in, as if it was drawing all by itself. Mother Freedom was lying on a mat of . . . leaves? Well, something soft, maybe pine needles. Yes, she was outside among pine trees. Behind the trees was a big kettle on a fire.

That kettle and the cabin it stood in front of reminded Anna of someplace. Her gaze drew closer to Rosalie, and to the hand that was pulling back from her side. There was a long, thin metal instrument in that hand, with two parts that closed together at the bottom, like metal fingers. They were pulling out a . . . Anna drew a bullet.

Now at last she looked at Rosalie's face. The eyes were closed. Rosalie could have been dead!

No, I won't stop here! Anna insisted to herself. Not now! She started another drawing.

There was the cabin again. And what were those skinny things on the ground? Chickens! Now she saw an old dog curled into a ball on a footpath.

"I know this place. Why can't I remember where it is? Where is Rosalie? Where's Rafe?"

A bucket appeared near the front of the drawing. "Why am I drawing this?" Anna wondered.

Anna made a new drawing, just of the bucket. For some reason she drew it from looking down over the top. Rafe's face was in the water! He was smiling. He looked so proud of himself! Anna had to laugh. "Rafe, are you . . . are you sticking your *tongue* out at me?"

At the sound of a door opening downstairs, Anna

bounced from her room, shouting. "Kevin! Mom! Dad! I just heard from Rafe!"

"You mean he *telephoned?*" cried her mother, hurrying up the steps.

"No. Well, yes, in a way."

"In a way? In what way?"

As the family piled into her room, Anna held up the drawings and began explaining. But the growing disappointment on their faces made her stop.

"Oh, my dear sweet girl," said her father. "We have to learn how to get over this together."

Anna gritted her teeth. "You don't understand. These aren't just drawings." She could see in their faces that they didn't believe her. "I'm sorry I showed these to you."

"Don't be," murmured her mother, trying to embrace her. Then she gazed at the drawings again. "This could certainly mean something, I'm sure."

"What?"

"Well, there are times when an idea just pops into my head out of nowhere, and I wonder where it could have come from. Then I discover that Allan had the same thought across the room. We try to figure out who had it first—who sent it and who received it."

"Mental telepathy, right!" Anna's father exclaimed. "Who knows? Maybe messages *can* be sent from one century to another."

"Especially when Anna and Rafe have lived in both."

Her parents tried to sound upbeat, but they left Anna shaken just the same. And if these really had been messages out of the past, they soon stopped. Anna wondered what it all meant.

TWELVE

As soon as Dora Terwilliger's elderly aunt Ida heard of the terrible events at the Terwilliger Hotel, she hurried from her Kentucky plantation to be with the family. Early the morning after she arrived, Aunt Ida had a very private conversation with Hanna's father. Sitting close together over a little wicker table on the porch, they drank the old lady's raspberry tea and spoke in hushed voices.

"I've made many searches for Hanna. I've looked everywhere in the woods for miles," Amos Terwilliger said grimly. "All I've ever found was some dried blood down by a creek. But that could have been left by Mrs. Sims, who we know was shot, though she too has now disappeared. So has her son, Rafe. The blood could just as well have been his—that poor, sad-eyed little boy."

"No one has helped you?"

"Not really." He picked up one of the cookies that his missing daughter had always loved. It got as far as his lips, but then he set it down. "The sheriff only pretends to be interested. He and the U.S. marshal here are much more interested in finding something to arrest us for."

"What I don't understand is how very alone Dora is here. This is a mother who has lost her child! Why doesn't anyone come to spend time with her? Don't you two have friends and people who believe as you do in your precious cause?"

"Yes, but if they showed themselves just now they too

would be watched by the investigators from the Southland Property Owners Association."

"All this because of *one* colored woman?"

"They certainly hate that one colored woman enough. But those investigators think they have a good chance now to find out where some of the other freedom stations are. They want to spread as much fear as they can so that our movement will die out from lack of help. They use private detectives and trackers. Now, with this terrible Fugitive Slave Law, they are able to put money into the pockets of northern judges to send any runaways they can find back to the South to face punishment, torture, and even death."

"Just a moment. I am not interested in hearing you talk about how inhuman the slaveowners are, being one myself. You mentioned the Southland Property Owners Association. A member of my family just married Austin Pembroke, a congressman from Kentucky. Unless my memory is failing me, Austin is the head of that association. Are you telling me that he had something to do with what has happened to our Hanna?"

"His group put up the huge reward for Mother Freedom. And on the day of his wedding, he made threats to Dora. He said he knew what she and Rosalie Sims were up to, and that the hotel was already being watched."

"Knowing all this, Dora *still* went on trying to spirit that little colored boy away from his owner. What is his name? Rafe?"

"Mrs. Sims's son, yes. You must know that your niece is very brave."

"Brave, or *stupid?*" Aunt Ida had been fidgeting with the spoon in her cup. Now she gave it such a hard clink that the fine china nearly broke. "Well, let us put that aside. The point now is that Hanna is missing . . . and probably worse."

"Yes. Our not knowing whether she is dead or has been abducted and taken somewhere is destroying Dora as well."

"I know. This is most horrible. Horrible."

"Then I have a favor to ask. There is *one* person who Dora is certain can shed some light on what happened to Hanna. She lives—"

Aunt Ida waved her hand. "Don't tell me you too are going on about that Conjure Woman! Dora has already spoken to me about her. My niece is desperate and will grasp at anything. I had hoped that you would be more level-headed. It is perfectly ridiculous to put stock in anything that some fortune-teller said. I know that she made a prediction that something was going to happen to Hanna. Dora told me the woman's words. They could have meant almost anything, including that the child was going to come down with whooping cough! Something always happens to children. That's how these people rope you in and get their claws into your purse."

"Believe me, I feel much the same way you do. But for Dora's sake somebody has to talk to the woman. If I'm followed there, she could be mistaken for part of our underground network. But these agents surely know who you are. They would hardly suspect you."

"I should certainly hope not!"

"Then would you consider—"

"Your wife already asked me, and I said no. Then I said I'd think about it. Now you're not even giving me a chance to do that. My sakes, I am eighty-six years old. Do you think I should let myself be pushed around like this?"

124

"No."

"Good. I'll do it. Not that I'll take any mumbo-jumbo silliness from that trickster, you understand. I just want to see if that woman really is over one hundred. If she is, I'll eat my hat."

"I'm very grateful."

When Amos bent to kiss Aunt Ida's hand, she glared at him. "It is completely clear to me that none of this would have happened if you hadn't made a pair of fire-eyed abolitionists out of Dora and my grandniece."

Dora stepped from behind the doorway. "Aunt Ida, that is so untrue! You of all people know what the women of our family are like. How can you blame *anything* that we do on the men?"

THIRTEEN

In the days before Aunt Ida arrived, the slave trackers had been very busy. Bo and Calvin had burned down the minister's church and terrorized his flock, but after days of false leads they had not found him. In frustration, their uncle had sent Calvin back across the river to fetch a pack of bloodhounds. Meanwhile he and Bo set up a night-and-day watch on the doctor's house. But neither the doctor nor Running Deer ever went back to where Rosalie Sims was hidden.

One morning while Bo was following the doctor on his house calls, his uncle followed his nose to the open kitchen window. Running Deer was inside baking. He politely tipped his hat.

"Mmm-mmm, I think I smell apple pie. That's one of my favorites, you know. Sure does make a feller's mouth water."

"Why don't you just go away!" Running Deer shouted at him. "One of you camps out here every night. The other follows my husband on his house calls. Don't you see that you're not going to get anywhere with us? Can't you leave us alone?"

"Might be I'm a-goin' to do just that, if Calvin gets back today or tomorrow with the hound dogs. It were a big mistake fer me to wait so long to send fer 'em."

"Hound dogs are hardly going to do you any good after all this time."

"Oh, they kin pick up a scent, don't matter how long. Ain't no dogs that I ever seen do it better. Besides, I got that blanket Rosalie Sims was a-layin' on when we carried her down to the courthouse. We kept it out of the rain pretty good and those bloodstains are still on it. Some of her smell is still on it too, I reckon."

"I don't believe you."

"Sure you do. You look into my eyes and you know I mean business."

"Even if it were true, she'd be well on her way to Canada by now."

"Oh, I don't think she's a-goin' anywhere while the roads are being watched so close. Agents are lookin' into every wagon and carriage. That's 'bout the onliest thing them fancy men who got hired by the property owners association are good fer. It's me and the boys gonna find the woman. The boy, too."

"He is dead. I told you that before."

"Show me where he's buried and let's go dig him up then."

"You did enough to him already. I won't let you disturb his grave."

"You are a powerful good liar," Uncle Daniel said with a slow smile.

"And you are even better at hating."

"That's where you're wrong. I'm a businessman. Now, I want to make a trade with you. Lead me to the woman, and I'll forget about the boy, and the preacher too. Also, I won't do another thing to her, jest turn her over for trial back home and collect my reward money. But somebody else is gonna think that she is too much trouble alive and kill her for sure. Is it a deal?"

"I'm in no position to make a deal. I don't know anything about it."

"Tell you what. I won't follow you this one time. You go to her and you talk it over. If she loves her boy, she's gonna give herself up."

"I wouldn't have any idea where to look."

"Listen here," Uncle Daniel shouted. "I ain't dumb. You helped break her free. You know where she is. And if you don't help me to get her back the easy way, I am goin' to kill them all! The law is on my side! Do you understand me good?"

"There's nothing more to say." Running Deer slammed the window down, but he hovered outside. What weapon could she use if he broke in? What?

Bloodhounds! she told herself, wringing her hands. They're coming today or tomorrow! How do I get away from him to go and warn them? How? *How?*

Running Deer stared at the wood-fired oven. Of course, the pie, spiking it with something in her husband's medicine cabinet. Something that would put him to sleep for hours.

Not very many miles away, Aunt Ida was getting ready to go see the Conjure Woman. She needed two things before she could ride off from the hotel. One was for someone to draw her the way to the cabin in the forest. The other was for Dora to have a talk with Joseph, the slave who had driven her from the plantation.

"I saw a strange look in his eye earlier this morning," Aunt Ida said. "He was fixing his own breakfast in the kitchen and he didn't even offer to serve me any. And look how he's staring at us now from down by the stable. Why, I wouldn't be surprised if he just runs off and leaves me with the carriage—or takes that, too."

"Just a minute," said her niece, ducking back into the hotel lobby. She came out again with a jar of ink, a writing quill, and an official-looking sheet of paper.

"What in the world is this?

"It's called a manumission document, Auntie. You just fill this out and sign it in front of witnesses and Joseph is set free."

"Why, you had this ready for me? Do you actually keep these documents around the house?"

"All the time!" Dora said brightly. "Now do be a darling and sign it."

"My sakes, isn't my word good enough?" snapped Aunt Ida. "He can't read anyway."

"Then he'll learn on this. What could be better?" For the first time since Hanna was lost, Dora actually smiled.

A few minutes later, Aunt Ida watched her niece go over to the stable and begin speaking to the slave, a young man of about twenty. Then Dora walked back, shaking her head.

"Are you going to tell me," exclaimed the old lady, "that I just freed him but he isn't happy?"

"Well, he's no different from you and me. Let me ask you how you would feel if you were leaving behind a mother and a father and two sisters who couldn't be free too?"

Aunt Ida rocked back in her chair. "This is too much! You don't fool me. I see that twinkle in your eye. I'm doing you a favor and you blackmail me?"

"My, what an interesting word for this."

"I don't think it's funny. In the first place each slave is worth a lot of money these days. You tell me, how am I going to run Fairweather Valley when I had thirty-four slaves just ten minutes ago and now there'll be only twenty-nine?"

"Twenty-nine?" said Dora. "Well then, there are thirty more left for us to free."

"Thirty? Why thirty?"

"Because, my wonderful auntie," said Hanna's mama, kissing her cheek, "you need to be free of this yourself."

Aunt Ida and Joseph were deep in the woods when Joseph pulled the horse to a standstill and climbed down. He opened the carriage door and said, "Miss Ida, I thinks we got trouble."

"Why?"

"There's somebody on horseback there who just stopped too. I'd been wonderin' 'bout him from time to time. But now I know fo' sure. We bein' followed. 'Scuse me a minute." He walked slowly away.

"Come back, Joseph. Don't you do anything foolish!"

The well-dressed man on horseback was the same investigator who had sneaked through the hotel searching for the hidden room. Watching Joseph coming up, he unbuttoned his long-tailed jacket.

"Boy, what's your problem?" he asked, bringing his hand back to rest near a fancy holster.

The gun's silver handle flashed in Joseph's eyes. "Good day to you, sir," he replied with a big smile. "My mistress sent me back to ask you if you has trouble with your horse."

"Why?"

"Because I be mostly a stablehand and does a lot of horse doctorin' back on the plantation. It 'pears yours must be lame to keep you so slow on the road. She be most happy if I was to look at this fine animal's hoofs and hocks for you, sir."

The investigator studied Joseph a moment and grew thoughtful. "I must say, that's mighty kind of her," he declared at last. "Go ahead."

Joseph felt the man's eyes on him as he bent down to lift the big stallion's front right hoof. He pretended to inspect it and the ankle too. "No, dis one is good. No cuts, no swellin'." He went around to the other side.

Twirling one end of his mustache, the investigator looked down and said, "I believe I've seen that carriage before, boy, on the other side of the river. Is your mistress Miss Fairweather, of Fairweather Valley?"

"Oh, yes, sir! And she do keep it shiny and clean. Dis here leg is good too. I go check the hind ones."

"I've heard about her troubles over her missing niece."

"Thank you fo' your interest, sir. That be her grandniece."

"Yes. No doubt she must be broken up about it."

"She sho' is. But she angry, too. Dis leg is all right."

"Angry? What about?"

"Oh, it's a family matter, sir. I shouldn't of spoken 'bout it like I just did."

"Tell me something honestly and I won't repeat it to anyone," the man said. "This just has to do with a bet that I made. While you're here with your mistress in the north, I imagine you must give some thought to running away?"

"Run away? Oh, no, sir. Not me," Joseph said. "Miss Ida, she trust me, and I ain't breakin' dat trust."

"Well, I'm glad to hear that."

"Thank you, sir! Well, I believe your horse is all right.

Maybe he just comin' down with somethin'. The horses get to know when dey need to rest. Got mo' sense then some peoples do."

"That could be." Dipping into a pocket, the investigator brought out a small coin. "This is for your trouble."

"Oh, no, sir. My mistress wouldn't have me take a thing. I thank you fo' the offer, though."

"So is she just out for a ride this morning?"

"Well, she goin' down to the post office to mail some letters."

"Surely on a nice day like this she'll be going somewhere else besides?"

"I 'spect so, sir, though she didn't tell me nothin'. She might want to see the town and the farms and such like that. Only . . ."

"Only what?"

"Well, 'tween you and me, it's them abolitionists. She don't agree with them no way, no how. Makes her so mad, I think she fixin' to leave real soon." Patting the horse, he quickly slid two fingers under the saddle. "Good-bye to you, sir."

"Good-bye, boy. She's lucky to have you."

Joseph walked away, muttering under his breath. "Yes, sir. You goin' to find out why just as soon as you press your legs into that horse's sides."

"My word," said Aunt Ida as he returned. "What's going on back there?"

"Back where?" asked Joseph, grinning, and he climbed up in the driver's seat.

"That man's horse is bucking all over the road."

Joseph looked over his shoulder. "Yes, ma'am, I do believe that's true." He shook the reins hard. "Giddyap! *Move!*"

When Running Deer came out of her kitchen with pie and coffee for the tracker, all the hard lines of his face gave way to a big smile. "Why, thank ye kindly," he said, as he took the plate and cup from her hands. "Ye surely surprise me, a-bringin' this out."

"I wouldn't let even you go hungry."

"You got a good heart." Squatting down by the campfire, he jabbed at the pie with his fork and put a piece in his mouth. "Say, this pie is kind of spicy. What's in it?"

"Oh, a touch of cinnamon."

"Cinnamon, that's it?" His eyes stared into hers again.

"And a sprinkle of ginger," Running Deer added.

"I see, it's the ginger then! Well, I like it, and this coffee, too. But you best git on into the house a-fore a chill takes you. It ain't all that cold, but I see you're a-shivering some. Don't worry 'bout the plate and the cup. I'll set 'em both down on the porch when I'm finished."

"All right."

Running Deer went back into the house. Once on the other side of the door, she put her ear to the crack of it, waiting.

There was a slow groan. Then a gasp. "Now what in tarnation!" she heard the tracker say. "What's she done to me? Why, that pie was pizened! I cain't see straight. Git my rife. Git my . . ."

Running Deer heard him stumbling around outside, muttering about what he was going to do to her. Now she heard his staggering footsteps coming up the steps. She heard him at the door. He leaned on it. He pounded on it. Then she heard his body crash to the ground.

Running Deer found him lying outside. She forced herself to bend over him to pry the gun from his hand. It went off as she tugged at it. The bullet must have singed his horse's ear, for the animal let out a frightened cry and galloped off. She might have taken it along with the rifle, but there was no chance of that now. Instead she dashed on foot into the woods.

No sooner had she gone than the tracker sprang lightly to his feet. The pie had gone uneaten, one piece spat out, the rest thrown in his campfire. His little scheme had worked. Now she would lead him to Mother Freedom. His mare had turned back and come nosing up to him, but this was a job to be done on foot. Running Deer could too easily spot anyone coming after her on horseback. She had taken his rifle, but a lot of good it would do her, since she'd left behind the powder horn and bullets. Meanwhile, he had the revolver he'd taken off Rosalie Sims, with five good bullets in its chambers.

"Give her a little more time," he murmured to himself while biting off a chaw of tobacco. "Don't want to folly along too close after my reward money."

FOURTEEN

Aunt Ida arrived at the Conjure Woman's first. The carriage rattled down a narrow dusty road that ended at a footpath. On that path sat a toothless old dog that set up such a howl, Aunt Ida had to cover her ears.

"I hate all this," she cried. "I hate it, just hate it. My back aches, my poor carriage is filthier than it has ever been, and my ears are ringing like church bells on Sunday. Can't you kick that dog and make it stop?"

Joseph shook his head. This was somebody's warning alarm, and he was not going to mess with that. But he did take the old lady by the arm when they set out on foot into the woods.

From behind a tall rock, a pair of eyes was watching as they went by. Rafe's small hand dipped into a bag that was full of David-and-Goliath stones. Beside him crouched the minister, holding a log like a club.

Rafe stared at that white lady's face. He thought he knew it, yet he could not say how until he imagined the smell of her cookies. Why, he had seen her face so many times! It was on the locket that Hanna's mama wore, and it was on the painting in Hanna's room.

Rafe knew at once that she had come to find out what she could about Hanna. He was so excited that he was about to call out to her, but the minister yanked him by the arm, warning with his eyes that they must be careful. It was only then that the boy reminded himself: Aunt Ida had slaves.

After Aunt Ida and her companion had gone by, Rafe ran down to the dog, telling it by a pat that it could stop howling now. Then he went softly down the path to see what would happen.

"How do," said the Conjure Woman, looking up from her boiling kettle.

"All right, I guess," said Aunt Ida. "How are you?"

"Oh, tolerable, thank you. Is you lost?"

"Not if I have come to the fortune-teller, I'm not."

"Well, I ain't a fortune-teller, so I guess you is lost. But befo' you go lookin' some mo', would you like a cup of sassafras tea?"

"Thank you, but—"

"Oh, the cup is clean. Got a chip in it, that's true, but you jest sip from the other side. Whyn't you set you'self down? I knows this here hickory chair don't look too strong, but neither does you and me."

"Thank you then, I will. This is Joseph, who is my . . . he used to be . . . well, he is a free man."

"Oh, I kin see it in his eyes, Lord be praised."

"Yes, well, be that as it may, I want to explain why I've come."

One look at Rafe, who was peeking from behind them in the bushes, seemed to have answered that already. "Something to do with Hanna," the Conjure Woman said. "Her mama cain't come to me, so she sent you."

"Why, yes! How do you know who I am and why I'm here?"

The Conjure Woman looked at Joseph instead. "Nobody follow you here?" she asked him.

He shook his head.

136

"You sure 'bout that?"

"Mrs. Terwilliger ask me to look out in case somebody might be. They was, but I left him back at the main road."

"Good. But maybe we stop the visitin' so you don't has to stay here too long. The child is all right. Her name Anna now, 'stead of Hanna. She live in Rochester, New York. The family that took her in like she was their own is named Post. She doin' drawings now. She want to be an artist sometime. One day she gonna draw your picture so she can have you there to look at for always."

"I don't understand."

"Well, the inner eye does it all."

Again she glanced past them at the boy in the bushes. "I'm sorry, but I got a feelin' that's bothering me. You be going now. Joseph, please take the—"

Suddenly the watchdog began howling again. Running Deer, panting and pushing the rifle in front of her, burst out of the woods on the far side of the cabin. Before she saw the strangers, she was already crying out. "No matter how Mother Freedom is, we've got to move her! They're calling in bloodhounds!"

"Running Deer, you is being followed."

"But that couldn't be! I made sure—"

"The dog ain't howling at you. Li'l Rafe, you stay there in the swamp mist."

"But there ain't no swamp here!"

"They is now!" She thumped her cane on the ground and a mist began to steam up around him. "I'm movin' the skip-over place to here."

"Wait! Wait!" Rafe cried. "Is you sendin' me into that other time?"

"I sho' is! That 'bout the only one of my tricks gonna protec' you. It the only way you be safe."

But Rafe rushed away from the thickening fog, crying, "No! Not without my mama goes with me!"

From a secret place in the pine woods came a weak and muffled cry, "My wonderful son, go on now. You do like she say."

"No! No!" Tears streamed from his eyes. "Oh, please, let me fights them too. I came back to be with you forever and always."

Moving shakily and slowly, Rosalie Sims appeared. She was very weak, and much thinner, and her hair had turned as gray as an old woman's. But in a voice as strong as always, she said, "I be with you in some other way. You has to live on fo' me. Cain't you see that?"

"No, Mama," Rafe sobbed. "Don't make me go."

"Yes, go now, my precious son."

Through all of this, the dog had been howling. Now it made a gurgling sound and fell silent. Quietly the tracker stepped into the clearing with Rosalie's six-shooter in his hand.

Running Deer whirled on him with the rifle. "You'd have to get my powder horn afore you could fire that, I reckon," the tracker drawled. "But go ahead, I'll give ye a first try. Now, folks, I don't want to kill nobody lessen I has to. I'll jest borry me that horse and carriage outside and take my two prisoners."

Joseph had been edging closer to him all this while. But the tracker was well aware of it. He brought his arm around to fire.

Just as he was pulling the trigger, Rafe's flying stone hit

him on the side of the head. Joseph was on top of him in a second, and they crashed to the ground. When the tracker was lying very still, Joseph took the gun from him and got up. "Is he dead?" he asked.

Aunt Ida was as pale and fluttery as a ghost. Still she managed to say, "If he is, I'll stand by you."

Running Deer examined the tracker. "No, he's alive. Unconscious. There could be a brain concussion."

"Lift him up, Joseph," said the Conjure Woman. "Throw him in the skip-over place."

From his mother's arms, Rafe cried, "Is he gonna wake up?"

Running Deer nodded. "Most likely."

"Then don't do that to the future. There's some of it that I'm remembering, and they sure don't need any more like him there."

"I'm afraid there's no help for it," declared the minister. "There's too much trouble he could make for anyone here who stays behind."

Aunt Ida looked at her driver. "That certainly would mean you, Joseph. Do you want to come back with me to Fairweather?"

"Only if I'm still a free man."

She gave him a sharp look. "It's on paper. I keep my word. Finish up with that trashy fellow on the ground and let's get to the carriage." She took a few steps and turned. "Rafe? Is that your name?"

"Yes, ma'am. I'm Hanna's friend."

"Don't you think I know that by now? Come along with me."

"With you?"

"Yes. Do you think I'm going to leave Hanna's best friend

139

here in trouble, especially when you have so much to tell me about her? You will be free, don't worry about that."

"Go along, now," said Rosalie, opening her arms and gently stepping back to let him go.

"I . . . I cain't, Aunt Ida. I cain't go without my mama."

"Now, who said you would? Naturally, she is a little bigger to hide. But there are shades on my surrey, and one of you can hide on the floor under my foot blankets. I'm sure we could manage. Don't you think so, Joseph?"

"I do, but . . ."

"But what?"

Running Deer spoke up. "Maybe he's thinking of the agents for the slave owners association. They're stopping everything going north. The sheriff and the marshal are helping them. They've been bought off."

Aunt Ida turned to her. "Are they stopping anybody going to the ferry?"

"I don't know."

"Well, it certainly doesn't seem to me that they would. Why should anybody expect that Mother Freedom—my word, what a name!—would be escaping *to* a slave state? Kentucky is the very one that made her an outlaw."

Rosalie stared at her. "Why you do that for us?"

Aunt Ida waved her hand. "I can't answer. If I had to, I might decide not to, so don't even ask me. One of these days I'm sure that you'll get together with Dora and *she'll* give you an explanation. She has all sorts of them at her fingertips." Pausing, the old lady stared around at one and all. "Don't any of you think that at my age and with my background I have suddenly become a fire-eyed abolitionist. Nothing could be farther from the truth."

Turning to the Conjure Woman, she added, "If you could make me up a package of those teas you spoke of, I will be glad to buy them. Does anyone know when the ferry leaves?"

"Usually it goes back an hour or so after it comes here from the Kentucky side," Running Deer said.

"Oh, then it will be quite late in the afternoon. Do you know the Terwilligers?"

"My husband does. He's the town doctor."

"I'll give you a message for them."

"Not in writing."

"Yes, I suppose you are right. Have him tell my niece . . . hmmm . . . tell her I said, *Dora, if I have gone bad, it's all your fault!*"

FIFTEEN

The ferry was still crossing to the Indiana side of the river when Joseph drove the carriage down to the landing to meet it. He had wiped all the dust off the carriage, and it shone like new in the last rays of the afternoon sun.

The old lady sitting inside did not look as if she was feeling well. The curtain on the window facing the setting sun had been partly closed to keep the rays of light from hurting her eyes. And although the day was still warm, she seemed to have come down with a chill, for she was bundled from head to foot in blankets.

The blankets were spread out over the rest of the seat— and over Rafe, as well, who lay there with his head in her lap. They flowed down her legs, which were stretched out over Rosalie, and onto the floor.

A well-dressed man with a huge mustache rode up beside the carriage. Aunt Ida saw his open jacket and the silver-handled pistol in its holster. He tipped his hat to her, but it was to Joseph that he growled dangerously, "You played a fine trick on me back there, putting a burr under my saddle."

"Don't you badger him," snapped Aunt Ida before Joseph could start trying to wriggle out of it. "What he did was my idea. And I hope it will teach you a lesson not to make a pest of yourself."

"Now see here, Miss Fairweather—"

"No! I don't feel well, and I do not care to see here or see there or see anywhere else. How is it that you know my name and are unaware that I am related by marriage to United States Congressman Austin Pembroke? He is, if I am not mistaken, the founder of that Southland Property Owners Association which pays your salary. If you continue to annoy me and menace my servant, Austin Pembroke will hear of it through a letter from my lawyer telling him that his new bride, Amanda Fairweather, has been cut out of my will. She will inherit nothing—no land, no money, not even those jewels she is so mad for. Now please remove yourself. I bid you good day."

Rafe, listening under the covers, could tell that the man was not moving. Very carefully he slid his hand down to his mother. What he touched instead was the cold metal of her six-shooter.

Aunt Ida may well have been very tense too, for she sounded as hard as that gun. "Do you have any further business with me?"

"No," drawled the man slowly, as if he was thinking things over, weighing one thing against another. "No, I think not. May you have a safe journey."

His horse turned and trotted off.

The ferry had been coming closer all this time. Now Rafe heard someone on shore nearby begin to shout. "Hey, Calvin! I cain't find Uncle Daniel. He left his horse, but he's gone."

"Talk louder!" came the reply from out on the river. "These dogs is a'-fussin' all over me, and I got trouble hearin' you. What about that horse?"

Bo, the slave tracker, got up from the log he'd been

resting on and cupped a hand to his mouth. "I say his horse is still where he was a-campin'. The fire's been out for hours, and I cain't find him nowheres."

"What did the doctor's woman say?"

"She says she don't know nothing 'bout it. But I think she's lying."

"Well, don't you worry. You know he can take care of hisself. Got to tell you, Uncle Daniel was right to make me take along this blanket with the stains on it. They been a-smellin' it and a-smellin' it, and they are dead set to go. It got 'em primed real good."

"Hot diggety!" cried Bo. "We goin' to be *rich*."

Now Rafe could hear the heavy, excited breathing of big dogs. "Well, this time I ain't counting my chickens afore they hatch," called Calvin from very close by.

Within moments the barge thudded softly against the wooden boards of the landing. The dogs could be heard yipping and jumping wildly about.

"Mama, is you going to shoot them if they come right at us?"

"Hush, now," whispered Aunt Ida, sternly. She stuck her head out the window as a man with a red bandanna around his head started to go by. "Ferryman, why are you going away? I need to leave for Kentucky right now."

"Sorry. You got to wait. I ain't a mule."

"I understand that. But I'll make it worth your while."

"Lady, I'll still be a poor man no matter what you pay me."

"Then please be a gentleman. I'm not feeling well and I need to leave right away so that I can get home without having to ride all night."

"Lookee here, you want to swim across? Go and do it. Otherwise, wait." Tugging at a bottle in his back pocket, he walked to the end of the landing and disappeared into a little shed.

"Don't jest stand there, Bo! Come over here and give me a hand gettin' these critters off! They feel like they're gonna tear my arm off a-gitting away from me," Calvin yelled.

"Be right there."

The slave tracker went by, giving the carriage a quick lookover. Calvin let down the gate of the ferry and the dogs tore away from their masters.

The wild stampede shot right by the carriage—but only for a second or two. Suddenly, the dogs whirled around and were throwing themselves at the doors and windows.

"Calvin, what's all got into them?" cried Bo, hurrying back.

"How should I know?"

Joseph, meanwhile, called out to the two men desperately. "Oh Lordy, gentlemens! Please don't let them scratch up all that fine shiny wood. I'm goin' to ketch it so bad if this don't stop."

Aunt Ida added to the din, shouting, "Joseph, if there is anything wrong with my beautiful surrey that can't be fixed, I am going to have the overseer bullwhip you till the skin is off your back! Now, you drive this carriage onto that ferry right this second!"

"But, Miss Ida," said Joseph, "that ferryman ain't ready to leave yet!"

"I don't care if he is or not. If you don't get going this instant, I'll come out and drive the carriage myself."

"No, mistress, no. Don't do that. Giddyap horse!"

By this time the ferryman was out of his shack, running

and shouting, "Stop it! You stay there. Don't you steal my ferry!"

He ran past the confused trackers, but the jumping, baying bloodhounds at the end of the landing blocked his way. Aunt Ida stuck her head out of the carriage calling, "Joseph, take the pole and push off."

But he was on his knees at the end of the barge. "Got to untie it first!"

Before Aunt Ida could push Rafe back inside, the boy sprang past her. "I'll do that," he said to Joseph. "You get the pole."

Joseph did and pushed off. As the ferry left the landing, one of the bloodhounds leaped aboard, racing for Rosalie behind the open door of the carriage. She raised her gun to fire. Before she could, Joseph's two arms wrapped themselves around the dog's belly from behind and heaved it into the water.

Rafe, meanwhile, had picked up the long pole, but there was little he could do with it. The barge started to drift. By now Bo was pointing his rifle at him as he and Calvin waded out to the barge. Rafe ducked back for his rocks, leaving Joseph to swing the pole at them.

Joseph worked the big oar, with Rafe trying to help him. Meanwhile, Rosalie stepped out of the carriage to cover them with her pistol.

For all Joseph's strength, he knew little about working a ferryboat. But the current was helping them now, carrying them downstream to the west and spinning them out toward the center of the river.

Crrrack! A distant shot sent a rifle bullet whistling past Aunt Ida. She hastened into the carriage, but another bullet crashed through and went out the other side.

"Is you all right?" Rosalie asked.

"I was a little girl the last time anyone shot at me, and then it was arrows, not bullets. But yes, I think so. Let's hope they've stopped shooting, though. It does not do wonders for my heart."

"Oh, I wouldn't worry 'bout your heart none," said Rosalie with a thin smile. "I think you just 'bout as strong-hearted as your niece."

"Dora was a Fairweather before she became a Terwilliger."

"I'm also thinking 'bout Hanna."

"You're squinting while you're thinking. What are you looking for?"

"'Cause the last time we crossed it, there were other trackers going up and down the middle of the river in boats to catch runaways—and looking for Mama too," Rafe explained.

"Don't see any now, though," said Rosalie. "Not yet, anyways. We goin' to make the shore anytime soon, Joseph?"

Aunt Ida was staring at the boy. "I declare, I've only heard you speak a few times, but the way you do keeps changing. Sometimes you use words as if you've had some schooling. And you look to be about seven or so, but there are times when you seem older to me. I suppose I'm just a confused old lady. Anyway, if I could get you to stay with me on my place, I could teach you everything I taught Hanna's mama. Maybe you could convince me about that skipping over."

The two women exchanged glances, and Aunt Ida added, "Well, I'd like to spare him, you know."

"Yes, I know." Rafe's mother put her hand on her son's shoulder. "But life don't work that way too often, does it?"

"No, it doesn't," said Aunt Ida, sighing softly.

Rafe went to her and took her by the hand. He could tell that she was thinking of Hanna, missing her.

It was in the hour before stars began to come out that they touched shore. The ferry glided over reeds and a bank of mud and came to a stop. They were in Kentucky, but where?

This was a question that couldn't be answered yet. First they had to get the carriage rolling through the mud and up a slope to a road.

The narrow road ran close to the river in places. A little farther on they saw a barefoot white youngster in coveralls, a pipe in his mouth and a fishing pole hanging down over a long rock.

Rafe went up to him. "Where is we at, do you know?"

The boy looked him up and down. "Course I know."

"Kin you tell me?"

"Shore I kin tell you."

"So what is it?"

"Why do you want to know?"

"So I kin tell where I is."

"Listen here, is you a slave?"

"No. How 'bout you?"

"*Me?* Now that's hardly likely."

"I feels the same way about it. Hardly likely. Well, so long."

Rafe was just walking back to the carriage when the other boy called. "Harristown is down the road thataway."

Rafe stopped. "How long it take to get there?"

"Depends on how long you stand around here asking questions."

Rafe started to walk away.

"Now that you're a-goin', I reckon you might get there afore the moon comes out."

"Well, thanks."

Back inside the carriage, Rosalie brightened. "Harristown? Well, we did some lucky drifting. There's a family of Quaker farmers I know of there. Dora and me worked with them time to time when there was somebody we needed to send north a different way than across the Ohio."

"Fine. We'll go there," Aunt Ida said.

"Well, not all the way," said Rosalie slowly.

Aunt Ida glared at her. "Surely you don't think that I'm going to give anybody away *now*. Why, I'm a culprit myself!"

"Not if you say I held this gun to your head. And that's what you *will* say, 'cause you cain't come with us."

"I have no intention of going with you! I have property to take care of. A big farm to run."

"Slaves to set free," Joseph called back to remind her.

"Well . . . that too."

"I'll show you where to let us off."

"Without Joseph?" Aunt Ida asked in alarm.

"No, he have to take you."

Mother and son got out of the carriage in the dead of night. Rosalie gave Joseph directions. Good-byes were said, and there were hugs before the carriage drove away. Rosalie and Rafe were alone now, listening to the fading hoofbeats. Then there were only the crickets and themselves.

"Why didn't you want them to bring us all the way to the farmhouse, Mama?"

"Because of Joseph. Ain't nobody gonna bullwhip Aunt

Ida to make her tell. They kin suspect her all they wants to, but she still one of their own. With Joseph it's different, and they could do him very bad. Though Lord knows that Aunt Ida could make anybody miserable who'd try that. Well, we'd better move. There's still a ways to go if we're going to get to the Quakers before sunlight. Rafe, you goin' to like them folks."

Walking slowly, hand in hand, they found another path. Until this point the moon and stars had given them enough light to see their way. But this other road was narrow and thick with trees on both sides. They had to move along carefully, step by step in the dark. But Mother Freedom knew this road. Just another mile or so ahead was a farmhouse where a single candle always flickered to light the way for any fugitive.

Rafe now held her hand in both of his. It was such a strong hand, and so gentle, too. He raised it to his lips and kissed it, then looked up into his mother's glittering eyes.

He was so happy.

SIXTEEN

As the weeks went by, Anna tried to fill in what she didn't know about those she had left behind. She had made many guesses, but there was no way to know for sure.

Anna's imagination was like the ocean—it came rolling in waves that picked her up and carried her along for a while. Then the wave would crest, and down she'd slide into that hollow and empty place where it seemed that nothing new would ever come again.

She was at the bottom of just such a slide when the phone call came that changed her life. In a voice that sounded strangely familiar, a young man said, "Excuse me. I don't know if I've gotten the right people or not. This may sound strange to you, but I've been making calls trying to find anyone named Post who can help me. This is kind of expensive, because I'm calling long-distance from Toronto. Do you know if way back in your family there was anybody who helped to run the Underground Railroad during slavery times in your country?"

"Yes, Amy and Isaac Post," Anna answered promptly. "Who's this?"

"Well, my name is Rafael Bonaventura. I'm a student at McGill University, and I'm doing a paper on the smuggling of fugitives up here to Canada."

"Oh, that's wonderful," said Anna enthusiastically. "My dad is writing about Rosalie Sims, who was called Mother

Freedom. Or at least he *was* writing about her until he ran out of material. She used to smuggle slaves out of Kentucky."

"Yes, I know."

"But nobody could find out anything about her after 1850. Wait a minute, did you just say that you know?"

"Well, I ought to. She was my great-grandfather's grandmother."

"Hold it, hold it. But your name is Bona—"

"That was the name of the man Rosalie Sims married up here. Her son changed his name too."

An electric bolt ran through her. "You're a descendant of *Rafe Sims?*"

"Sure I am. How would you know about . . . oh, wait a minute," he said excitedly. "So that story about your family Bible is right! I didn't believe it. That's the problem with history being passed down by word of mouth. You never know where it got changed around."

"Wait, please. What about the Bible?"

"Well, Rafe used to tell his children and his grandchildren—"

"He had children and grandchildren?"

"Listen, that's kind of obvious, considering that I'm on the phone."

"Okay, I see what you're saying. You'll have to excuse me, I'm a little bit . . . never mind, go on."

"He would make up stories about having traveled through time and lived in the future. He really had people convinced. Of course, when they grew up they realized it was impossible. Anyway—"

"Excuse me," Anna interrupted. "In those stories, did he ever say anything about someone named Anna? Or Hanna?"

"Why?"

"No reason."

"You sure?"

"Well, my name is Anna, all right?"

"Okay."

"Anyway, never mind. You were saying something about a Bible?"

"Yeah. He said that his mother had become very sick again by the time they got as far north as Rochester, so the Posts hid them in their attic for a long time. Meanwhile they helped Rafe with his reading and writing. Before he left, he put a little letter into the family Bible. He said it was for the future. I'm not sure what that meant. But I figure that you know about the letter . . . or maybe it was a poem. I'm not sure. Anyway, he signed his name, so that's how you'd know. Am I right?"

"Not exactly . . ."

"You sound as if there's something you're not saying," Rafael said. "You could tell me anything, believe me."

"Well, it's only that you remind me . . . I mean, you're older, but you almost sound just like . . ." Anna's voice faded in confusion.

"Who?"

"Nobody. It's just some craziness in my head. Listen, can you tell me how Rosalie and Rafe got away from the trackers who crossed the Ohio River into Indiana?"

"The trackers? I can't believe this! You know so much about my family already. Well, first they went into Kentucky—"

"Into? Are you saying *into*?"

"That's right. The roads going north were blocked, so they hid in an old woman's carriage and she took them on the ferry. Only—"

"Wait a minute," Anna interrupted. "Don't you mean a woman in her thirties, whose aunt lived on a plantation on the other side?"

"No, I think she was somebody's aunt, who'd been visiting and now was going back."

Anna's voice grew hushed. "Was the somebody . . . was she called Aunt Ida?"

"Yes, that's it. She had a last name like Fairvalley."

"Fairweather! She owned Fairweather Valley!"

"Then you've heard of her," Rafael said in wonder.

"Yes!"

"Well, all right! I mean, fabulous! This is great!"

"You say she took them back into Kentucky?"

"Well, not before there was a gunfight on the river."

"My aunt was shot at!"

"Your aunt?"

"Forget it, I'm just getting too excited. Sometimes it's just like I was living then, you know."

"You ought to go into teaching history, if this stuff gets to be so real to you."

"I'll think about it. Tell me if she . . . was anybody hurt?"

"No. Once they got to Kentucky, Mother Freedom knew where there was a farm nearby run by some religious white people who were in the fight against slavery."

"They were Quakers," Anna said.

"Oh, this is too much! So you know about them, too?"

"Well, I never met . . . I mean, I've heard about them. Go on."

"The Quakers kept them there for, I don't know, some days. Mother Freedom was really weak because she'd been shot. But I don't mean on the ferry—"

154

"I know, I know," Anna said impatiently.

Rafael grew even more excited. "You do? How do you know? I mean, did the Posts leave any notes and things that are still in the family?"

"Well, no. Not many. I'm not even sure about the Bible. I think we have an old leatherbound one, but I wouldn't know how far back it goes. I'll look for it right after we talk. But how did Rosalie and Rafe get out of Kentucky? Did they go back across the river to Indiana?"

"Oh, no. It was some adventure, let me tell you. The Quakers got them to the next station on the Underground Railroad. It was a really dangerous trip, because most of the time they were heading east through slave country. They even got on a real train once, when they were already in Richmond, Virginia, finally going north. They went in somebody's trunks, like baggage.

"Then in Washington," Rafael went on, "they were smuggled onto a boat that got them up to New York City. There they got onto another boat going up the Hudson River. Eventually they made it to Rochester, and then to Canada."

"Listen, Rafe. Sorry, I mean Rafael—"

"Hey, that's okay, you can call me Rafe. That's who I'm named after. I just use Rafael because it sounds, well, romantic."

"Rafe, do you know what happened to Aunt Ida? If she didn't go with them, did she get into trouble?"

"I can't be sure. All I know is, she went back to the plantation. She was supposed to have freed her slaves at some point, and her driver became very active in the Underground Railroad later on. They used to hear about him up in Canada."

"Why didn't anybody hear about Mother Freedom after that?"

"She wasn't all that well, and she wanted to spend time with her son. But she did what she could from up there—organized places for the fugitives to stay, and so on. In Canada you couldn't be too open about what you were up to, because it might embarrass the government. There was a lot of business going on between the two countries, and a good part of that had to do with cotton and tobacco from the South. Listen, I can't stay on the phone long. My budget is tight."

"Just tell me real fast about their going to Rochester. There were other jumping-off places for Canada, especially New England. So why did they go through Rochester?"

"Because it meant so much to Rafe. He kept talking about going there. When his mother asked him why, he couldn't explain. But he knew the name of Post, and he kept repeating it."

"This is taking my breath away. I can't tell you what it does for me," Anna exclaimed.

"You sound so excited. Listen, what college are you in?"

"I'm just in high school, but I would really like to talk to you more and to meet you. So would my family. Where can we get in touch with you? Can you come down here if we send you a bus ticket?"

"Oh, you don't have to do that. It's not that far. But if your folks could put me up—"

"Of course they would!"

They traded addresses and made plans. As they talked, Anna tried to imagine what Rafael looked like. The more she listened to him, the more she could hear something in his voice of *her* Rafe!

As soon as the call was over, Anna ran to her father's collection of old books and papers behind a glass door on his bookshelf in the den. Among them was an old leatherbound Bible.

Anna opened it carefully, leafing through page after page. It was just where the Bible began to tell about Moses bringing the children of Israel out of slavery in Egypt that she found a sheet of paper. It was dry and turning yellow. There were just a few lines on it, and they were so faint that Anna had to search through her father's desk for his magnifying glass to read them.

Anna could tell that someone had helped Rafe with his spelling, and there were a couple of small inkblots where he had pressed too hard.

Anna was having trouble seeing. She had to wipe away a tear or two before she could make out these words:

> There is a place in my heart
> When I lose my friend
> That the love go on
> And don't never end.

This poem is mine, Hanna-Anna. And I means it too. Good-bye for now. There is somebody here who will remember you for always.

Rafe Sims.

Check In to Mystery at

GHOST HOTEL

Anna, an adopted child, has always wondered who her real parents are. When Anna and her family check in to a strange old hotel, Anna meets the ghostly Colonel and Mrs. Terwilliger. Her resemblance to the couple's missing daughter is eerie—especially since the young girl disappeared over one hundred and forty years ago!

Unable to resist the lure of the past, Anna is drawn back in time to the danger-filled days of the Underground Railroad, which helped runaway slaves to freedom. Here Anna discovers the mystery of her childhood—a mystery that must be solved if Anna is ever to find her way home again.

ISBN 0-8167-3420-8

Available wherever you buy books.

Troll